About the Author

George Roberts is 40 years old and has been married for 21 years. He has two adult children who now tower above him and remind him daily. George loves to write but the most enjoyable moment for him is when he gets a new and fresh idea in his head for a new story, it develops slowly whilst he does the day-to-day chores and eventually makes it on to paper. George loves life and enjoys people. In his day job George helps to support autistic adults, a job that he finds extremely rewarding, although at times very tough and challenging.

Dedicated to my wife, Berni Spires. For putting up with me this long.

Best Wishes

Grace,

C Roberts

George Roberts

FROM TEN DOWN TO THREE

AUSTIN MACAULEY
PUBLISHERS LTD.

A CIP catalogue record for this title is available from the British Library.

ISBN 9781787101494 (Paperback)
ISBN 9781787101500 (E-Book)

www.austinmacauley.com

First Published (2017)
Austin Macauley Publishers Ltd.
25 Canada Square
Canary Wharf
London
E14 5LQ

Chapter 1

1986

Worcester Park, Surrey

His strong, young legs spirited him towards the goal as his muscles pushed him through every sodden inch of the waterlogged pitch. There was an onslaught of defenders in his way, each one vying to be the player to end this streak of footballing brilliance. A few clever twists and turns and then, with the goalposts that had seen better days just a few yards away, he deceptively dropped his head and turned the opposite way from where the opposition was assuming he would go. With one last effort, he struck the ball with precision and speed and all the keeper could do was watch as the ball bypassed him and landed perfectly in the net for the second time that afternoon.

A tremendous roar erupted from the sidelines as the final whistle blew. The soaking wet, freezing cold parents celebrated their team's victory yet again. James smiled to himself and walked tiredly over to see what compliments his dad had for him this time.

"Well done, James!" his father beamed.

"Thanks, Dad," James said as he reached for a bottle of water.

As he was about to take a well-earned gulp he was struck with an overwhelming pressure in his forehead and he dropped the bottle just before it had a chance to touch his lips. Water flowed from the bottle as it rolled through the air. His head fell forward and then his legs buckled, leaving him with nothing else to do but fall to his knees. His body fell to the drenched ground with a heavy thud. James started to panic as he desperately tried to move his head, his only view being the legs and feet of the people who were now gathering around him. The pure spring water pouring from the bottle was diluting the brown, murky puddle in which his face had fallen and, with each intake of breath, James battled to stop himself drinking it. Blades of floating grass were beginning to collect in the corner of his mouth, every exhaled breath causing the water to softly ripple. With his eyes seeming to be the only thing working, he could see the bottom half of his dad lunging forward.

"James! James!" his dad shouted, as he frantically dropped down beside him. "Can you hear me?"

Gathering what little strength he had, James blinked his eyes rapidly in answer and then closed them slowly as oblivion claimed him.

With light piercing his eyes and the noise of voices all around him, James woke up to a vision of pure whiteness. He tilted his head to the side and scanned his surroundings. The curtain surrounding his bed was slightly pulled back, enough for him to see his mum and dad talking quietly with a doctor. His dad turned around and noticed that James was now awake. He placed a hand on his wife's shoulder and jerked his head towards James and their conversation stopped immediately.

"Hello, James," his mum said. "How are you feeling?"

"I feel okay now, Mum. Can we go home, please?"

"Yes, of course. As soon as we can, I promise," she replied, as she placed her hand on his cheek and rubbed softly with her knuckles.

James did not understand what was going on. One minute he was a footballing hero and the next minute he found himself engulfed by total bedlam in a busy children's hospital ward. He did not know how long he had been asleep but now, being awake, he had no desire to stay here any longer.

"It's okay now, James, we can go home," his dad informed him, much to his relief.

"There seems to be nothing wrong, they said," his mum said as she tried to hide the uncertainty in her voice.

His dad started to pack away the few belongings that they had gathered together whilst James got dressed. Together, they walked out of the hospital with the relief of knowing that nothing serious had happened. At least according to a qualified doctor and who were they to argue? Things were simply put down to an allergic reaction to something as yet unknown.

The following day, James's mum made an appointment for him to see their GP. She was still uncertain and, after a sleepless night of worrying about James's health, she decided that a second opinion would be best.

***

"James, are you ready?" his mother called out to him.

"Give me two minutes," he shouted back.

James did not bother to have a wash before slipping into his jeans. He surveyed the chaotic heap of clothes that covered his bedroom floor and picked out a t-shirt that his brother had helpfully left draped over his trainers. Rushing downstairs, it was hard to believe what had happened less than 24 hours ago.

"Are you ready now?" his mum asked impatiently, watching him leap down the last couple of steps.

"Yep, let's go!" James replied with the twang of a false American accent.

The waiting room was unsurprisingly filled with sick people, with the noise of sniffing and spluttering being broken only by the occasional cough. Uncomfortable, high-seated settees were placed next to coffee tables stacked with out-of-date magazines. As James began to people watch he found himself focusing on a tiny, elderly lady. She had not moved since the moment James and his mum had got there and he started to wonder if she was dead. Trying to see if she was breathing, he leaned forward in his chair and narrowing his eyes he concentrated on her chest: not even her tan, cashmere trench coat was moving.

He slowly returned back to his original position, still fixated on the elderly lady. The young man sitting next to her suddenly emitted a loud sneeze, accidentally knocking the side of her leg.

"*Phew!*" James thought to himself as she casually opened her eyes, adjusted her body, and pushed her false teeth out of her mouth and straight back in again.

She noticed James staring at her and she smiled at him pleasantly. Without waiting for his return smile she closed her eyes and fell straight back to sleep.

"James Squires!" a deep voice suddenly called out.

James did not see who said this and, with the grip of his mum's hand gently tugging at his wrist, they walked through to the doctor's consulting room. As they passed a nurse James could see that it was her that had shouted out his name not 10 seconds ago. He mischievously looked up at the stubbly-chinned lady with a hint of confusion. Realizing that James was grinning and about to laugh, his mum awkwardly pulled him towards her. She looked down at him and gave him a look of consternation which he interpreted in no uncertain terms: *Behave!*

As they got further away and out of hearing distance from the unwomanly female nurse, she bent down to James's level briefly and whispered the unusual word to him: "Steroids."

Not completely understanding, and in his own head imagining the robots from *Star Wars,* he naively giggled to himself. He was not entirely sure how the two fitted together but he still found something quite funny in the whole situation.

"Hello, James, take a seat," said the doctor, as he leaned back in his chair behind his desk. "So, what seems to be the problem?" he asked in typical doctor style.

James's mum explained everything in great detail, including a few things that James had never heard before. She wanted to make sure that everything was covered and that they had every opportunity to find out exactly what was wrong. That was *if* there was anything wrong, of course. Maybe it *was* an allergic reaction to something as they had been led to believe the previous day.

The doctor pulled his feet along the floor and effortlessly set the wheels under his chair in motion. He rolled towards the light switch and with a quick flick he turned it off, leaving just the dim lamp glowing in the background.

"James, please will you just look up and focus at that spot on the ceiling," the doctor instructed, using his special torch to indicate the spot to which he referred.

He glided towards James and eased himself close so that their faces were almost touching. James could feel his warm breath brush across his nose. The smell of garlic from last night's dinner made James feel a little bit queasy. A few grunts and a positive nod later, both James's eyes had been checked. The doctor stood up cheerfully and turned the light back on.

"I can't see anything there that concerns me and there are no obvious signs of pressure. My advice would be to try staying away from chocolate and cheese for a while. Let's see if that makes a difference," he preached convincingly.

There was not a lot that James's mum could say to that. She had to put her trust in the doctors again. With a little bit more positivity now, she looked down thankfully at James. The unknown was gradually becoming the known. She felt more confident and reassured now that in the last two days she had been given the same diagnoses from two separate doctors.

Chapter 2

1990

Quite a few things had changed in James's life. He and his family had moved to the Midlands, settling in Malvern. Although the headaches were just as bad as they used to be, and would quite often pop up just to let him know that they had not gone away completely, James had learnt to live with them. He never talked about them and he never let them get in his way; he was happy in his denial. He got used to the loud ringing in his ears, which at bedtime caused him to have an unnatural fear of sleep. But what is unnatural for others became the norm for James. He figured that nobody wanted to hear him moaning about the same thing over and over again so he stoically kept it to himself. In short, life went on.

It was late, much later than James and Chris were used to, and the sound of their whispering would have been heard if anyone had been awake.

"You grab the poster," Chris quietly ordered his brother.

"Okay. You check the door," James replied.

In his one hand James nervously gripped the poster that the whole prank revolved around, and the other hand prepared to gently open the door of their shared bedroom. He gently pulled the handle but immediately paused a moment to stifle the creaking of the unoiled hinges. Another attempt, but this time a little faster: one motion with a less abrupt squeak. With the door now open, they stealthily crept their way across the landing. The dog lifted her head from her basket and tilted it questioningly. She was confused to see the boys up at this time of night. They were almost there as they gingerly tiptoed across the floorboards, avoiding the ones that they knew would creak and groan under any type of pressure. James straightened up his bent and creeping body and made way for Chris. With the door slightly ajar, he pushed the bottom corner lightly with his bare foot. They were inside now and the well-planned operation could begin.

Removing his sister's jeans that were neatly hanging over the red plastic and metal MFI chair, Chris began to quietly move it towards the side of her bed. Once in position, he climbed onto the chair. Collette was a deep sleeper, but she would certainly wake up if her brother happened to fall on top of her. He balanced himself perfectly as he placed his feet diagonally on the corners of the chair. With the poster still rolled up, it suddenly occurred to James that this was a part of the plan that they had not thought through properly. He gently began to open up the poster, barely daring to breathe.

"Shh!" hissed Chris frantically as the paper began to rustle and potentially jeopardize the whole mission.

James passed up the poster to his brother while keeping one eye securely on their sister. He then stepped back with anticipation and watched Chris go to work. Looking down at James, Chris gave him a blank expression and, in the style of a crab's pincers, pressed his forefinger to his thumb repeatedly over one of the corners of the poster. Shrugging his shoulders and furrowing his eyebrows in confusion, James tried to read his brother's code. Chris glared at him and repeated his miming act and then, finally, the penny dropped. James tiptoed back to their bedroom and picked up a pack of Blu Tack.

With the poster securely up, Chris returned the chair underneath the white, chipboard desk while remembering to replace the white, ripped denims then peeked back quickly to admire his handiwork and then he followed James out of the room. Again, they crept over the landing and, learning from their mistake the

19

first time, swiftly closed their bedroom door behind them. They climbed into their separate beds at the same time and they excitedly waited until morning. But morning would come a lot sooner than they thought.

With only the sound of the ticking grandmother clock and a single chime to indicate 1 a.m., the dog awoke from her slumber. She lifted her head and pricked up her Alsatian-like ears. Leaving her basket in a frenzy, she descended rapidly down the stairs and raced to the back door. There, in front of her, she saw an intruder skulking in the shadows. Her low, rumbling growls quickly became loud barks, disturbing the peace of the night as she banged into chairs and chased her enemy around the dining room table.

The dog flew up the stairs in pursuit and she followed her foe into Collette's bedroom. Collette was awakened by the uproar and, of course, the first thing she saw was the poster of Pennywise: not a normal, happy, friendly clown, but the clown from Stephen King's 'It'. His razor-sharp teeth and evil eyes penetrated Collette's sleepy mind and she screamed as she felt the bed covers shake and then sensations of pain as sharp claws dug deep into her thigh. Raising the duvet away from herself in fear of her life, Collette watched with horror as the dog then leapt violently onto her bed still trying to catch her prey. With the dark room filled with screams, hisses and growls, Collette pushed herself far into the corner of her bed, the pillow her only means of protection, covering her face and hiding her tears. She was absolutely terrified and it was a wonder she did not wet herself.

"What is it?" her dad shouted as he threw open the bedroom door.

"D-dad, th-there's som-something in m-my r-room!" Collette stammered shakily.

Her dad switched on the light and saw the dog crouched down beside the bed, staring fixatedly underneath it.

"Collette, get off the bed. Let's have a look," he instructed with apprehension.

He hesitantly moved the bed away from the corner and jumped back at the sight of a petrified ginger cat trying to make his escape by scaling the pink, flowery, papered wall. He began to laugh and then noticed Pennywise's nasty grin beaming down from the ceiling. Collette was relieved but shaken and her legs were covered in scratches and blood.

"Don't worry, Coll. I'll deal with them in the morning," he said grimly.

He released the uninvited houseguest outside and taped shut the supposedly unused cat flap, promising to himself that he would fix it at a later date, while Collette received exaggerated medical treatment in the bathroom from her mum.

Now, Chris and James could not have planned this better themselves. The timing was perfect. The cat had been a godsend, a practical joke to beat all practical jokes. They knew that they would suffer the consequences for this, but they thought it had been worth it. They did not get the chance to see the reaction on their sister's face, nor did they feel the pain of what she thought was Pennywise's claws breaking the skin on her legs in a demonic frenzy, but their imagination was all that they needed. The next morning they were not so brave, however, and they were understandably a bit wary of going downstairs.

Walking down the stairs to meet their fate, James whispered to his brother, "This is a week to two weeks' grounding, I reckon."

"How do you know? We might never leave the house again!" Chris replied.

"Because I know everything."

This was a phrase that Chris was used to hearing over the years.

"Yeah, that's right, James. I forgot; stupid me," he said as he walked down the last step.

As they were bombarded with accusations, Chris muttered the immortal words, "I'll take the fifth."

It was something he had just learned at school, but he obviously had no idea what it meant and it certainly did not apply at this moment in time. From the moment he uttered that ridiculous phrase, things went from bad to worse. As their parents' angry voices grew louder, the grounding went from one week to two. Collette stood and smiled in the background. Her smirk turned into well-rehearsed tears when their mum and dad turned to her to showcase her injuries as good reason for such a harsh punishment.

After the grounding had finished and they had served their sentence in good spirit, all James and Chris wanted back was their freedom. That afternoon they had arranged to meet up with a lad called Kevin. They never actually liked Kevin that much: he was the boy who had everything and the boy who would never share. As part of the package, his little brother would always tag along with his goofy teeth, blond hair, and permanently fixed gormless grin. James always wondered how strange it was that Steve had blond hair yet Kevin's was black and curly. James thought perhaps one of them might have been adopted.

Kevin and Steve were pretty lucky in the way that if they wanted something they got it. A new pool cue, an air rifle, or a bike – you name it, they got it. Today, Kevin had a brand new set of golf clubs. James could never remember Kevin even being interested in golf, but there, in a big, red Wilson bag, was the shiniest set of golf clubs they had ever seen. They all met up at the Americans, which was a massive field right by their houses and ideal for a round of golf. Chris and James falsely started to admire Kevin's undeserved clubs.

"Hey, get your hands off! You can look, but you can't touch!" he barked.

Chris and James looked at each other and raised their eyebrows in unison. It turned out that Kevin was actually quite good at golf and could hit the ball quite far. Chris and James watched and walked, watched a little bit more and walked a little bit more, following the ball wherever it landed and, bit by bit, became Kevin's caddies.

"Let's have a go, Kev," James asked politely.

"No way! Dad'll kill me. If you break them, I'm dead!" he retorted quickly; a well-practised response that had been drilled into him from the day he was born, no doubt.

James never asked again, but when he and Chris got home it was all they could talk about. They both wanted a new set of golf clubs.

"Do you boys know how much golf clubs cost?" their dad asked with exasperation. "A lot of money, that's how much!" he continued, answering his own question.

The following day, their dad pulled up outside in his bright blue Lada. He stepped out of the car and went to retrieve something from the boot. In his hand were five golf clubs: a driver, a 1-iron, a 4-iron, a 9-iron and a putter. He excitedly walked up the garden path and unlocked the door.

He enthusiastically called through the house, "Boys, I have something for you!"

James and Chris ran excitedly through the back door from the garden and into the hallway. At first, their excitement was obvious. But, when they were handed the clubs, on closer inspection they were dismayed to see how worn and battered the clubs actually were. One was made out of wood and one was curved in all the wrong places. Nevertheless, the 4-iron, 9-iron, and putter all looked pretty good. Although they were a bit disappointed they were never ungrateful so they thanked their dad with the typical kiss and cuddle, drumming up as much enthusiasm as they could muster without it being obviously put on. Leaving the two inferior clubs behind and clutching the new bag of golf balls, they headed back to the Americans.

It did not take long for both the boys to realize that golf was a lot harder than they had first thought. James managed a few good hits and could drive the ball from one goalmouth to the other but Chris could not get the hang of it at all. He pushed the tee into the ground and placed the ball on top. With the ball now ready for take-off, Chris lined up his first shot. He then practised his swing. James could tell that this was not going to be a pretty sight. With the club now perfectly lined up to the ball, the shaft was shiny and it glistened in the sun as it drew back ready to make its quick descent...

"Oi, Chris! Where'd you get those, then?" an annoying, childish voice rudely shouted, breaking his concentration.

Kevin and Steve were strutting cockily across the field. Steve was wearing his trademark Newcastle United top and gormless grin, relishing in his new role of caddy, and Kevin was wearing a newly acquired pair of yellow, checked golf trousers, with a glove strategically placed in his back pocket and his new, white golf shoes reflecting the sun's rays superlatively. Chris stopped his swing in mid-flight.

"That's all I need – Rupert the Bear and Bill Badger!" he whispered in annoyance.

Too embarrassed to admit that their dad had actually gone out and got the clubs, James made up a story about how the clubs had been found in the shed. He stammered every word of every sentence. It was obviously a lie and he fooled no-one.

"Go on then, Chris. Let's see what you can do," Steve jokingly requested.

Holding the club behind his neck and resting both arms over each end, Chris replied, "Nah, you're all right, mate. I was just about to go home."

"No, you weren't. You were just about to have a shot," Kevin said, producing an 8-iron from his recently washed down bag.

Not seeing any way out of it, Chris acted as professionally as he could while James was already thinking of ways to excuse himself from the proceedings. With the ball still in place, Chris began once again to take aim. The club whistled beautifully back through the air and gracefully back down again. James was quite impressed, until Chris's knees started to bend and he moved his left foot back just before impact. The club plunged hard into the dry soil and it snapped in two pieces of equal length. Left just holding the handle, Chris began to laugh. He knew that this would be the reaction of Kevin and Steve so, to save his own blushes, he thought that he would get in there first. Still laughing falsely at his own actions, he decided to make a move and go home. James followed suit immediately, picking up the broken club as quickly and as discreetly as possible on his way. When they were out of sight they looked at each other and laughed hysterically together.

A few days later James decided to have another bash at golf. One of his dad's mates ('A friend of a friend of a friend,' he said) had kindly welded the 4-iron back together and he set off, yet again, for the Americans. He desperately hoped that no-one would be there to see him try to hit the ball with a club now sporting a curious bulge halfway down it.

It was not long before James realized that, in order to strengthen the club, the mystery welder had placed a small metal rod within it. This meant that every swing resulted in the clang of steel against steel, creating another possible situation to cause more unwanted laughter.

Not long after James had dejectedly thrown the golf club into the brook that surrounded the park, Kevin hopped over the stile and into the field. Wearing the latest Liverpool kit and holding a bright orange, brand new Mitre football, he began to start his own private kick-about in the field. People turned up from nowhere at the sound of a boot against leather and, before he knew it, Kevin had initiated a full-on game of football.

Pigeon Eyes turned up in his usual attire: grubby trainers that had seen better days, grubby, unwashed jeans, and a grubby, off-white sleeveless t-shirt. No-one knew why he was only known as Pigeon Eyes. No-one knew his real name and, curiously, his eyes looked perfectly normal. But one thing that everyone *did* know was that he was always within spitting distance of trouble. His brother, another unknown quantity and sporting an unkempt mullet haircut, was the friendlier of the two, but his reputation still preceded him. Rumour had it that at the age of 14 he had been expelled from school for punching a teacher. Not one person had any proof of his expulsion and neither did they know if he had actually hit a teacher but, just like all the others,

James was always too scared to ask him about it. But one thing was certain: the one with the mullet sure could play football.

Pigeon Eyes rarely played the game, but, instead, he was always content to hang about in the background, either climbing trees or torturing any unfortunate small animal that he happened to find. As he trudged through the stream searching for trout, he found James's discarded 4-iron sparkling beneath the icy, cold water. He plunged his hand into the brook in wonderment and grabbed it with urgency, running his fingers up and down it as though he had struck gold. Drying his hands on his jeans, he gazed happily at his new toy. With his typical brutish behaviour, he began to verbally threaten the old oak tree that was situated right in the corner of the park.

"Stupid old tree!" was shouted repeatedly at the tree that had stood there unharmed and harmless for hundreds of years.

He persisted in hitting it over and over again, the noise of pipe inside pipe only adding to his depraved pleasure. After a while, and after wondering what else his new-found toy could be used for, Pigeon Eyes started to throw the club high up into the air. Relishing this new game and watching the velocity gather as it fell through the air, he challenged himself to launch the club higher and higher as every landing created a deeper divot in the ground.

As James continued to play football he could see Pigeon Eyes looking up to the sky waiting for his weapon to land. Then he saw Pigeon Eyes shield his not-very-pigeony eyes from the sun and violently twist to the ground, landing in a crumpled heap.

"Um, Joey, I think you had better check on your brother," James said, passing on what he had just seen.

"Damn, not again!" Joey called out, as he rushed over to his now unconscious sibling.

Pigeon Eyes had thrown the club into the air and, in his wisdom, had decided to try to catch it, but, being hindered by the sun and his own stupidity, the club head of the 4-iron had created a large dent in his face. With Joey now racing to his brother's aid, James and his friends continued to play football. They were not terribly interested and did not really want to get involved.

James always used all of his skill, agility, and speed to conjure up a few tricks and, on this occasion, one in particular – a manoeuvre that he had learnt from watching Ossie Ardiles in *Escape to Victory*. Everything seemed at that point to flow perfectly in slow motion with the sound of sirens in the background adding to the effect of the moment. As the ball came within striking range, James skipped passed Kevin. Balancing on his right foot, and with the perfect amount of pace, he kicked the ball with confidence. An orange blur flew through the air and clipped the underside of the crossbar.

Steve had no choice, but to concede the goal and he threw his new pair of Nike goalie gloves into the goalmouth dust, cursing profusely.

Passing the ambulance and walking into the park, Chris drifted along as he chatted with a lad called Daniel. Daniel was a few years older than Chris and James and for some reason had taken a disliking to James. He was good at football but every time they played together James would get the better of him. James did not like him too much either. It was most likely jealous rivalry that caused the friction between the two of them.

James saw Chris look in confusion at the arrival of the ambulance. He glanced back a couple of times and saw Pigeon Eyes wailing and being stretchered into the ambulance.

"Don't bother asking, Chris. Pigeon Eyes has broken his face. All right, Daniel?" James reluctantly asked.

"Got room for two more?" Daniel asked.

James mentally shrugged to himself at Daniel's lack of response to his greeting.

"Yeah sure, you can go on my team, Dan. Chris–"

But James's decision was cut down with a hostile attack from Daniel, "Sod that! You can have Chris, and I'll go on the other team."

James knew that Daniel was spoiling for a footballing skirmish.

"Okay, mate, whatever," James replied without taking the bait.

As soon as Steve had blown his imaginary whistle the game restarted, but this time with a little more competition and a lot more aggression. Every time James received the ball Daniel was there with a savage shove or an unprovoked elbow to James's now rapidly bruising ribs. In strength and power James did not stand a chance, but, with his cleverness and dexterity, he could upstage Daniel just like he had done so many times before.

This time, however, there seemed to be a little more malice in Daniel's play. The ball moved across the discoloured grass; a 50/50 chance for either James or Daniel to get there first. James instinctively challenged towards the ball with Daniel destined to meet him from the opposite direction – James having both eyes on the ball and Daniel having both eyes on James. With no attempt to win the tackle, Daniel used his whole body with all his force to throw James across the field. Shuddering through the air, he landed headfirst onto the hardened soil. Chris watched in horror as James lost consciousness. Daniel spat, sneered, and watched. His anger now released and his vile job done, he coldly paraded away. He never looked back once as he vaulted over the stile. He had been there for one purpose and one purpose only.

***

"James, can you hear me? I'm Dr Silver. I want you to lie still while we scan your head."

With his eyes flickering open and shut, James could see himself being processed through what looked like a giant Polo Mint. A red dot of light flashed on and off as it revolved around a black dome. Shadows moved from left to right and synchronized perfectly with the clunks and whirring and buzzing noises that got increasingly louder.

"James, it's Dr Silver again. You're okay; this won't take long. Just try to relax for a few more minutes."

James mouthed to himself, "Okay."

He wondered if he could be heard from inside the scanner but when no-one spoke again he assumed not.

"What the *hell* is happening?" he asked himself out loud and very crossly.

"We're just taking pictures of your brain, James. That's what's happening," an amused voice replied.

He now realized that he could indeed be heard and said, "Sorry, I didn't think you could hear me!"

"That's okay. Your mum's here with me and all is fine."

"Oh sh… I mean… *Sorry!*" James stammered with embarrassment.

After having his scan, James was checked over for concussion. He felt sick and was physically tired, but, surprisingly, he was allowed to go home. No sooner had they all arrived back at the house, the phone started to ring.

"Bob, will you get that?" James's mum shouted as she pulled off her coat.

"Hello? Okay. On our way," James's dad said into the receiver. "We have to go straight back to the hospital," he relayed in a worried voice.

As all three walked through the blue roadside gate and up to an old part of the hospital James's mum was overwhelmed by doubt and confusion and she was starting to fear the worst. Although all around her seemed normal, the sound of the road just yards away and the people going about their normal day-to-day routines, she started to get a sinking feeling deep down inside. This, somehow, did not feel right.

"Ah, Mr and Mrs Squires. Do come through. James, will you please wait outside for just a moment?"

James waited and watched as his parents disappear behind a bright white door, tapping his feet in rhythm to the beat that he played in his over-imaginative head. He waited for what seemed like hours, but was, in fact, only a few minutes. The door eventually opened and the doctor gestured for James to enter. He timidly walked towards his parents and noticed that his dad had been crying. James had never known his dad to cry before and his anticipation and fear started to build.

He anxiously sat in the gap between his mum and dad, nudging them along as he did so to make room for him. He looked fleetingly into his dad's eyes. He then turned and did the same to his mum; neither could hold his gaze. James's dad removed himself from the settee and away from the room. He could not stand to hear what the doctor was about to repeat. Holding back the tears, he walked right up to a wall in the corridor. Leaning his forehead and clenched fists against the wall, the tears began to stream steadily down his face. After his initial shock had died down he gathered his thoughts and began to try to come to terms with what was happening. Crying would only cause James more anguish and confusion.

He had to be strong for his son, but how could he do this? How could he find the strength?

He did not have the answers, but he would have to find them, somehow. They would all have to find a way to cope with whatever the future was about to throw at them as a family.

"James …" The doctor paused, as if struggling with what he must say. He cleared his throat and started again. "James, my name is Mr Giles. I have been asked to explain to you the scan results that you had earlier today."

"Okay," replied a bewildered James.

"The scan results show that you have a growth in a part of your brain which is called the cerebellum. This part of the brain controls a lot of things, like balance and coordination. If you can imagine an orange and that orange is placed in a bath of water, the orange would cover the plug hole and prevent the bath from emptying. This is sort of what you have in your brain."

"Okay," James repeated flatly.

The doctor pressed on, "The only way we can remove this growth is with a small operation."

"Okay," said James for a third time.

The doctor went on, but by this point James was not listening. He could see the man's lips moving, but he could not hear what he was saying. The words become one long, meaningless drone. He went into a world of his own. Each touch from his mum's shaking hands just passed on all of her insecurities so he shrugged her off. He just wanted to go home. He needed the normality of his family back. He had never asked for any of this and he did not want it.

It was not long before something began to change in James. His vulnerabilities turned to courage and his despair became belief. Although he did not quite understand what was happening, he somehow knew what he had to do. His young life was about to reveal a terrifying new chapter.

Chapter 3

James was lying on his hard, robotic bed as he looked around the ward. His mind was going into overdrive. This was something he had only ever seen on the news and during the yearly event of *Children in Need*. All around him he could see sick children. Children with no hair, children covered in scars, babies that cried for their parents' comforting touch. James felt bewildered, but he was not scared.

The first things that started to affect him were the heat and then the noise. There were children of all ages, with James being the eldest there. Screams of pain and discomfort merged with the sounds of laughter. Night-time was the worst for James, though. The uncomfortable sweat became worse with every turn of his body, with sleep becoming a distant memory as the other children cried in unison. Hourly checks were carried out with military precision, aided by the penetrating light of a nurse's torch, and they did nothing to help him settle. James rolled away from his mum, who was sleeping upright in the chair beside him and, for that first night only, he silently cried himself to sleep.

He was rudely awoken the following morning by a little girl who was shrieking and wailing. Her mother tried her best to console her, but to no avail. It was not the little girl's fault; she was obviously in a lot of pain and at the age of only three or four she had no other way of expressing her anguish. She would always be the first one awake in the morning, only to scream until everyone else had woken up, too.

James would pass her many times as he made his way up and down the ward. He always gave her a smile and, with her curly blonde hair and bright, blue eyes, she would always return it with a lovely one of her own. James would get to know this little girl over the next few weeks. He did not know why, but he felt almost compelled to try to cheer her up.

One day, as he was walking past, he was drawn to the sound of her cry. The curtain that covered her bed was slightly open, allowing him to see what all the screaming was about. He could clearly see the scars that marked her young body. Some of the scars looked nearly as old as she was and some of them looked recent. They ran painfully across her tiny chest, with each one serving as a reminder, as she grew older, of the pain she had gone through and the courage she had shown each and every day of her life since the second she had been born. Even though she had lived nearly all of her entire short life in hospital, she still found the ability to laugh and smile.

James walked slowly towards the gap in the curtain and gently pulled one aside. At only the slight noise of the plastic curtain rings sliding across the metal rail the little girl turned around and looked up at James. He just smiled as he had done before on many occasions, but this time there was no return smile. James could see that she was on her own. He knew that her parents were not far away; they never were.

"Hello, my name is James. What's your name?" he said in a soft voice as he stood next to her bed.

The little girl said nothing, but she had stopped crying, for the moment at least. James was almost speechless himself when, as he neared closer to the side of the bed, the scars that he had seen before became more magnified on closer inspection. He told himself to stop staring and tried again to talk to her.

"I bet I can guess your name," he claimed with a childish but reassuring smile. "I bet it's Laura... no, Lisa... no, wait... Linda?"

James looked at the young child and gave her a puzzled look. It was at this point he could see the start of what he thought could be the onset of a smile, so he continued. He was struggling now to think of more girl's names beginning with the letter L, so he started to just make names up as he went along.

"Is it Laboobin?" he asked as she began a smile that grew bigger and bigger as she shook her head. "Is it Latuba?"

Her head didn't stop shaking and her grin was now permanent. She leaned forward and grasped her cuddly, pink elephant that James always saw her with. With both her tiny hands she pulled it in against her chest leaving only a few scars visible to James. It was now only the tubes that rested on the top of her lip and continued up her nose that James could still see.

After a few more of James's seemingly pathetic guesses at her name she called out, "It's Lucy!" with a loud laugh.

"Well, that's just silly. I would never have guessed that if you hadn't told me. I would have been here all day!" he laughed and moved the crumpled bed covers at the end of Lucy's bed to one side and sat down.

Lucy fixated her bright, blue eyes on James, following everything he did from that point on. Her smile was now as big as the moon and whatever pain or discomfort she had been feeling was still there, but James felt like a good distraction. If that's all he was, a distraction, then that was good enough for him.

"Well, Lucy, I'm just here to say hello, so hello! While I'm here, though, we might as well have a little chat, eh?"

Lucy nodded and then began to twiddle her hand through the curls in her blonde hair, wrapping them tightly around her index finger, letting go to resemble a spring and then continuing the process all over again with another one of her locks.

"What's the name of your elephant?" James asked.

"Guess," Lucy replied.

"Do I have a choice?" he asked and then shook his head in unison with Lucy's.

Lucy finally gave in to James's outrageous elephant name guesses and blurted out, "It's Nelly!"

James could not help but smile to himself and at Lucy. Nelly was the most obvious name for an elephant but he never guessed it. Even Lucy seemed amused that he genuinely couldn't guess it.

When James first introduced himself to Lucy and entered into her world his first thought to start off any conversation with her was to be, "What's all the crying for?" That had all changed now after all the name games. He could now see that Lucy was happy. She wasn't crying, screaming, or squirming and she did not seem to be in pain, although she obviously still was, but it did not show for those moments that James was with her. He did not want to remind her of the pain or the reason why she was in the hospital in the first place. He wanted to be a person that could help her forget about the bad things and this is what he had accidentally managed to do.

He had not had a lot of experience with young children in his life. Not since he had become a teenager, anyway. Lucy was easy to talk to. She was so happy even though she was going through hell each and every day of her life. Yes, she cried a lot, but with that came a joy that James was unable at this point to understand.

Their conversation seemed to go on for ages and James never struggled to find any words or find ways to make Lucy laugh, even when her mother came back with redness in her eyes that could only have been caused by her last bout of uncontrollable crying – the crying that was always preceded by worry and then more crying, every single day.

With the nurses coming in to see Lucy it was time for James to go back to his own bed for a while but not before he promised to come back very soon. Maybe next time he would try to guess the names of the teddy bear that lay on the side cupboard and the toy penguin that sat upright at the foot of her bed.

James saw Lucy many times after that and every time he did it was the same: she laughed out loud and giggled quietly, and that smile – oh, that smile! – would fill James's heart with joy and hope every time he saw it. It didn't take long for him to realize that whatever it was that he was doing for Lucy she was doing exactly the same thing for him. She was making the worries, fears, and dread he felt every day dissipate. They just simply melted away every time he spoke with her. James was beginning to understand the power and impact a single human being, no matter who they are, can have on someone else's life. Lucy had made a huge impact on his and he was sure he had done the same to hers.

At only a young age Lucy was now someone James could call a friend. He made her happy and she made him happy. The innocence of a young child was clear to see in her eyes but cruelly and steadily that innocence was fighting against what she was learning every day, that life can be so hard and so painful. This is a heart-breaking lesson in life for anyone to learn, let alone a child as young as Lucy. When you still have the ability to smile and laugh like this young child did then you and your innocence are fighting back against all odds and you are winning, aren't you?

Opposite James slept a boy of ten years old called Mark and to the right of him there was a girl called Amy. Amy was just a little bit younger than James and she had recently undergone the same operation that James was waiting to have. She had had a brain tumour removed just over two months ago. James looked on, watching despairingly as Amy's mother spoon-fed her. Her weakened, skinny arms rested upon the blanket that had been freshly supplied because she had failed to make it to the bathroom on time. She could no longer speak, her words only being understood by her attempts at pointing, which were often misread. Her now disabled body needed help with every decision that was made for her. James prayed and hoped that this would not happen to him. There was nothing else he could do about it other than pray and hope for a more positive outcome for himself.

Finally, the day arrived when James's life would change forever, the date now etched in his memory forever: 10th October, 1990. At 10.30 a.m. precisely, James could hear the jubilant whistles as they swept through the ward. A middle-aged man strode towards James. His dreadlocks were barely covered by his hat and a couple of days' facial growth was beginning to show a hint of ginger.

"Hello, James. My name's Frank and I will be your anaesthetist for the day," he said with a cheerful wink; the humour being delivered with an authentic Birmingham accent.

This was the man who was about to start it all off. His would be the last face that James would see before he was sent off into an induced sleep – a whistling, Brummie hippy with a pocketful of powerful drugs.

As the bedridden James was wheeled through the ward he concentrated his focus on the ceiling, counting each and every light along the way. He had counted 12 as he was expertly manoeuvred around the corner. The doors swung open and his bed was pushed through and then they swung shut again, allowing James to briefly catch sight of his mum and dad one last time.

"Okay, James. I'm just going to give you a little something to make you sleep," the cheerful hippy informed him.

"Okay," replied James in a very small, frightened voice.

"You'll feel a little prick..." The hippy stopped midsentence as James began to smile at hearing the words 'a little prick', and then he continued, "It's amazing how many people still laugh at that! Anyway, you'll feel a little *scratch*..." He paused and smiled himself and then continued, "When I say so, can you try to count backwards from ten and see how far you can get?"

For some reason, James saw this as a challenge. He had convinced himself that he could make it all the way back to one and beyond.

As he got the go-ahead, he began to count in a strong, confident voice, "Ten, nine, eight, seven..." As his mind began to drift, his words started to come out quieter and slower, "... s-six, f-five... f-f-four... th..." and, with that, James fell asleep.

His mum and dad paced up and down the waiting room for what seemed like forever. They nervously

46

pounced on every medical person they saw, wanting news about their son. The hands on the clock did not seem to move and every second felt like a long, agonizing hour. They had never felt agony like it before. This was their baby and there was nothing they could do but wait.

James had been in a drug-induced sleep for just over seven hours. As he opened his eyes he was vaguely aware of his uncle's face leaning over him. His eyes could not focus, though, and after just a few seconds his heavy eyelids closed again. Each time he awoke briefly over the next few hours for just a few seconds a different member of his family would be present, creating a new memory that would last a lifetime.

When he finally came round for more than 10 minutes, his throat was very sore from all the tubes that had been shoved down there. He tried to talk but his words spilled out in an incoherent jumble and he still could not focus his eyes on anyone or anything for more than a second or two at a time. He became aware of a discomforting feeling travel from his toes and it did not stop until it reached his head. He tried to raise his arm in an attempt to show that he needed to move his body into a more comfortable position. He had lifted his arm not a few inches off the bed when it began to shake uncontrollably from side to side. The strength it took to move any part of his body just a fraction resulted in utter exhaustion.

James's parents, who had never left his side, called the nurse for assistance. With the bed bars now fully down, two nurses caringly adjusted James's supine body. It was then that he noticed the amount of blood on his pillow as his head followed his body that was now facing towards Amy. He was just like her now. He could no longer speak and none of his limbs could understand signals being relayed from his brain.

He was not ready for this! He had not been informed that he would end up like this: '*Just a small operation,*' he had been told.

"It will be all right, James," a voice that James did not recognize said, but he was too tired to see who it was.

Just before closing his eyes again, James took one last look at Amy and he drifted off to sleep.

As the days passed, with each one merging into the next, James started to feel that little bit stronger. He knew that he would need to fight hard to get back to normal – at least, as normal as he could possibly ever be again. Each new day brought new obstacles. He had to learn the basic things in life all over again, from reading to eating and walking to talking. In short, all the things that most people take for granted and never give a moment's thought about doing. The one thing that James was able to do freely for himself during his stint in hospital was think. He thought about many, many things.

He had found a new understanding about life and how precious it was, and how people take for granted how amazing their bodies actually are. He, too, had been one of those people until it was all taken away from him. He would no longer live that way, he told himself.

Mr Dockly was the man who had saved James's life. He was the man who had spent five hours removing the tumour from the brain of a person he did not even know. He would often walk through the wards, checking on his patients.

"James, you're looking a lot better today! How are you feeling?" he asked with an encouraging smile.

Managing the simplest of words by now, James was able to reply, "Better."

"That's great! I just need to speak with your mum for a moment."

James watched as his mum walked away from the bed as she listened to Mr Dockly. Then a strange thing happened.

"It's benign, James, so don't worry," a softly spoken woman said.

The words had come from inside his mind, as if he was thinking the words himself except he knew he was not. He knew that he did not have to reply and that he only needed to listen. His mum looked worried as she came back to speak to him. She relayed briefly what Mr

Dockly had just been telling her. They were waiting for some results to see whether the tumour had been benign or malignant. James's mum chose not to use those exact words, though. She waffled on about this and that, trying to pretty it up with meaningless euphemisms, but James knew what she meant.

"Don't worry, it's benign," James said confidently, although his words tumbled out slurred.

His mum looked back at how far away she had been standing with Mr Dockly. She thought about how quietly they had been speaking when that word was mentioned. There was no way that James could have heard them. Maybe he had heard it elsewhere? Maybe he had picked it up on one of Mr Dockly's other visits? She really did not know, but she did not question him about it. Instead, she smiled in wonderment at her son. The results came through the following day and the tumour had, indeed, been benign.

"Told you, Mum," James slurred with a lopsided smile.

"Yes, you did, James. Indeed you did," she replied happily, "It's a good result, James, a very good result. Things are looking good. It looks like luck is on our side."

Her comment touched a positive nerve in James. Not once did he ever feel unlucky during this whole situation. Lucky, yes. But unlucky? Never. He thought deeply about every little thing that had happened along the way, leading up to this. If his dad had not given him the golf clubs he would not have been in the park. If he had not been in the park that day he would not have played football. And if he had not played football that day then he would not have banged his head. It was the bang on his head that had actually saved his life.

James's thoughts then turned to the voice that he had heard inside his mind. He wondered if she was real or his own mind simply thinking, like everyone does. He was almost convinced that she was in some way real although he could not explain to himself exactly in what way. Whoever she was, his mysterious lady had been right in what she had told him.

The voice had been predicting his future. Or maybe not? Maybe she knew exactly what was happening. Maybe, just maybe, she had been with him all along, but this was the first time she had chosen to let her presence be known. The more he thought about it the more confused he became. Disbelief started to set in as James controlled his over-imaginative mind. He started to convince himself that the idea of someone watching over him was comforting but it was only an idea and nothing more than that. James heard the voice a few more times over the weeks, but the stronger he got the less he heard her. Sometimes, he tried to call her and ask her questions that he needed answering, but, gradually, she faded away altogether. At least, he stopped hearing her voice inside his mind. Although he could not hear her voice anymore, James had the feeling that she was still there in the background.

He was slowly starting to get better. The everyday functions returned to his body in stages and his eyes worked almost as well as they did before. He was glad to notice that he no longer had any of those excruciatingly painful headaches that he had accepted as par for the course for all those years. Although he had a very long way to go and he would still grudgingly have to accept help to bathe and get dressed, he knew inside that it would not be forever. And so he started to get use to hospital life. He was given food when he was hungry, a drink when he was thirsty, and his family was with him, but it still was not the same as being in the comfort and security of his own home.

From the corner of his eye, James could see two nurses pointing towards him as they walked in his direction. He knew exactly what was coming: it was bath time. He had already used his quick thinking to avoid having a few baths but this time he could not think up a single good reason to dodge the inevitable humiliation. Most of his body did not work as well as it had before, apart from one thing. His mind was every bit the same as any other red-blooded 14-year-old boy, and adolescent boys are not renowned for having great control of their wayward thoughts. It had not escaped him that some of the nurses were very attractive, especially the two who were dressing themselves in white, waterproof aprons in preparation of his impending scrub down.

He still tried to make his excuses, but they knew very well that he could not run away. Still in his striped pyjamas, they wheeled him away while his mum followed with his soap and towel. The nurses did not hang about and before he knew it his bottoms were being whipped down only to be left keeping his feet and ankles warm during the slow removal of his top. He felt the colour in his face drain as his testicles shrank to the size of peanuts. Nurse Susan got to her knees and started to pull his pyjama bottoms over his feet. Her head was just inches away from his delicate area and her mouth was moving as she casually began a conversation with his mum. James just sat there, watching her lips moving suggestively near his shrivelled penis. Her head nodded up and down, sending a million impure, but natural, thoughts shooting through his mind.

James tried to imagine anything he could to make the unhelpful thoughts go away. The steam settled over the slightly frosted glass and another possible distraction was taken away. This was the last place James thought that he would get the onset of a sexual thought, and he was mortified. He contemplated crying to get away from the situation but that probably would not have worked anyway, he realized.

He was steadied equally by both Nurse Susan and Nurse Becky as they lowered him into the water. He almost hoped that it was cold, but then his toe hit the warm surface. But the worst was yet to come. The nurses were good and thorough. They were intent on washing each and every inch of James's milky white body. His mum could see the worry now clear on his face as he sank lower into the bath.

"Do you want me to wash you, James?" she suggested unhelpfully.

"No!" James shouted in alarm, his voice breaking a little.

He had enough to contend with already and the last thing he needed was for his Johnson to get a mind of its own and come to life the second his mum took over the washing duties! The poor boy was in utter turmoil. Why did the nurses not understand that they were putting him through sheer hell? He did not need a bath, anyway. It was not as if he had been running a marathon or working out in the gym! In desperation, he thought of anything he could in order to stop the unwanted inevitable happening: old people, dead animals..., but nothing worked. Nurse Susan brushed over it, and his worst nightmare threatened to become reality. James snapped his eyes shut and, while desperately trying to control his panicked breathing, he started to count backwards from ten in his mind. He did not know why, but it was his last resort and at that moment it was all that he could think of doing.

"Hey, Sister wants to see you. I'll take over here," a male voice informed Nurse Susan in an effeminate way.

James had been saved from the clutches of despair. He did not mind what happened now, but he was annoyed with himself for not thinking about men in his time of need. His ever-wondering mind then came up with the notion that if he had thought of a man while his eyes had been tightly shut and his body was being rubbed down in soapy water, what would that have said about him? He had come into the hospital as a heterosexual 14-year-old lad and after having a brain operation he had turned into a homosexual 14-year-old lad. Maybe it was best that he had not thought of men, after all.

The following day seemed different, somehow; the ward was much quieter. James was not woken in the usual, familiar way by Lucy. He could hear people talking much more quietly than usual. This had never happened before. Babies would cry morning, noon, and night, but not today. What had changed?

James's mum arrived back from the bathroom, looking sad.

"You're going to find out anyway, James, so I might as well tell you," she said. She paused, thinking her words through carefully, before finally saying, "Lucy passed away last night."

His mum almost seemed guilty as she passed on the bad news and her eyes were still red from her tears.

"I knew something was wrong, Mum. I could feel it," he replied with sorrow.

James felt rage building up inside and he asked himself lots of questions for which he had no answers. Why did Lucy die, leaving her parents nothing else to do but think of their beautiful daughter every day for the rest of their lives? And all those what ifs: what if they had found a different treatment? What if she had held on a little bit longer and a donor had been found? And the worst thought that any parent could surely have: what if they had never had her at all? That must surely be a thought that would create guilt beyond any explanation possible, but the only scenario that would have spared their daughter any pain at all. There would not have been any suffering, any operations, and no scars.

Why does any child get sick? Why should some babies only get to see the sight of the same blue and white walls while their very existence is being kept going with only the aid of medication or tubes that invade every part of their fragile, little bodies?

James looked around the hospital ward. The majority of children were under the age of six –what had they done to deserve this? Nobody deserved this. Children should be playing and learning, their early years being guided lovingly and guarded by the people who created them. They should not be in here, or in a place like it. Life was not as nice as he remembered before he had been shoved cruelly into this reality.

People go through this kind of heartbreak every single day, all over the world. Yes, he had seen those television programmes that raise money for the very people he was now living amongst, but being there, slap bang in the middle of it all, sparked emotions that he never knew he had in him. He had to get outside and feel the fresh air. He needed to breathe it into his lungs and back out through his nose; a simple thing, he knew that, but an action, nevertheless, that he was longing to do.

His mum decided that it was best if she went and found a wheelchair, but James needed to walk; he wanted to do this on his own two legs. With his mum holding him tight under his left arm, James started to walk and each step proved to be practice for the next. With it being late in the year, car exhausts emitted fumes that became more noticeable on contact with the freezing cold air; something most people never even notice. James gladly absorbed it all, including the sound of people talking as they made their way to their chosen destinations.

James found it hard to understand how they could carry on as normal. Why were they not upset that a young girl had just died, not yards from where they roamed?

Seven extremely profound words then followed. They were words that would have an incredibly deep impact on James and help him to see life with a new perspective. The voice clarified what he already knew, deep down: "*Everyone has their own life to live.*"

That was the last time that James heard the mystery lady's voice. Her last words illustrated volumes through his mind which had been, up until now, confused and immature. He now understood so much more. Everybody had their own problems. Big or small, to them it was still a problem. He always thought that this was the type of thing that only happened to someone else, but now *he* was that someone else.

To the man walking across the road with his dog, James was that someone else. To the taxi driver who almost did not brake in time, James was that someone else. Lucy and all those other children who suffered daily were just someone else to somebody. It did not seem fair, but that was how it was. People are born and people die. That is the harsh reality of life and the only thing that anybody can ever guarantee; they just do not know where or when the end will come. Most people live in the comfort of believing that they will not get ill or they will not get that phone call to say that their life is now in the balance and they will never have to witness the things that James was seeing at this very early stage in his life.

This comfort, this cocoon, that had been brutally taken away from him and from every other child who was lying desperately in that hospital ward would be the one thing that any of them would struggle to find again, if ever. There would always be that insecurity that lingered deep in the back of their minds. Yes, they might be cured from whatever illness they had. They may be able to walk and talk again, but getting back that feeling of protection? Not so easy.

His thoughts provoked his imagination; an awareness of life well beyond his years. Where had Lucy gone? Had she actually gone to a better place? Surely she was not just born to die? Surely she did not just live in torment for those three short years of her life, in torture, only to end up nowhere? She must have gone somewhere. There are people out there who do evil things, like kill or rape, and they seem to get away with it. They live a full and healthy life. Where do they go when they die? They must get punished in some way. There has to be a Hell. There also has to be another world: a good world, a happy world, a world where no-one gets poorly and nobody dies. James liked the thought that this was where Lucy was now. No scars, no operations, and no more pain. James came to the conclusion that there must be a balance somewhere.

Chapter 4

James's grandmother was a little Southern Irish lady, hailing from County Clare. That afternoon she had decided to come and visit. This would be the highlight of James's five weeks stay in the hospital. She regally moseyed through the hospital wearing her claret, patent court shoes, the shoes she only wore on special occasions, and the heavy trench coat that she wore every time James saw her. Her blue-rinse hair was noticeable from afar as she stopped for directions halfway down the ward. An Indian nurse popped her head up helpfully above the desk, more than willing to lead the way and guide her to James's bed.

"Thank you," she said sweetly to the nurse and then, turning to face James with the nurse still within earshot, she casually remarked, "This place is full of them."

"Full of what, Nana?" he asked.

"Pak–"

"Mum, stop! It doesn't matter James," interrupted his mum, glaring disapprovingly at her own mother.

"Hello, James! How's your head?" she asked, scowling at her daughter who scowled back at her. "You really should look after your head, James. It's the only one you've got," his grandmother declared, as if James had somehow given himself the brain tumour.

Of course she did not actually think that he had. This was just how she was, not processing the words through her brain before they crudely passed her lips. James giggled to himself. He knew that his grandmother was not aware that she had made any sort of joke. The conversation got funnier and funnier. His grandmother was not what you would call politically correct, but the comical thing about it all was the fact that she did not know it. Her beliefs were deeply rooted and her remarks often offensive, but, in her own eyes, they were innocent.

The two women sat and chatted for a while. It was something that they did not get a chance to do very often so, for James and his siblings, this was nice to see. He relaxed back into his bed and liked the fact that good things can happen during unhappy times. His grandmother stayed for most of the afternoon, visiting hours being ignored for one day only. James was very sad when it was time for her leave. He wanted to make sure he did not miss a thing. He leaned forward and shifted his body, using his weakened arms to drag his legs over the side of the bed. With his feet dangling just above the floor, his mum helped him to put his slippers on.

James began to shuffle down the ward. As he passed the nurses' bay he made eye contact with the Indian nurse whose gaze had been following every step that his grandmother made. Her gritted teeth were hidden only by her attempt at producing a smile. She must have heard his grandmother's comments; they *all* must have heard her comments. James cringed with embarrassment as he looked away quickly.

Before she left, James's grandmother had a few more words of wisdom: "James, you'll be okay. I know it," she declared with confidence. "I knew a man once who was amputated from the knees up and he was fine."

James tried to stifle his chuckles, but with every attempt they only got louder until he was full-on belly laughing. The people resting quietly on the other side of the door turned their heads in an attempt to see what was so funny. The Indian nurse's head popped up as she pressed her face up against the round window and gawped. She scowled and shifted her eyes from left to right as she slid back down, the breath from her nose leaving two jets of steam behind on the glass. Her snorts faded as she stomped back to her duties. Unfortunately, this just made James howl even more.

"Mum, did you hear what you just said?" James's mum said to his grandmother.

"Of course I did. I can't see what's so funny about it," she replied indignantly.

James could not contain himself. His whole body moved backwards and forwards, resembling a character from inside a cuckoo clock. He rocked forward a little too far and his dad had to grab him swiftly before he hit the floor.

With her Irish brogue becoming stronger and her voice louder, his grandmother started to add reasoning to her claim: "It's true. His name was Geoff and he lived at the bottom of our road. He used to go to the pub with your father. He's dead now, mind you. Tragic, really."

"Bye, mum! See you soon," James's mum said patronizingly.

James's grandmother did not leave her house much anymore so, to James, her visit was an honour. Walking back to his bed, James made sure not to look in any nurse's direction. He kept his head down all the way. His mother, on the other hand, felt mortified and apologized to every one of them individually as she walked by in shame.

***

For the whole time that James was in the hospital, the one thing that he could not understand was his brother's attitude. The twin that was born just 10 minutes after he had made his own entrance into the world, the person with whom he had joked and laughed for the last 14 years. Every visit would be the same. The whole family would arrive in a convoy, each one giving James a kiss and a cuddle as they reached the bed – but not Chris. James knew that Chris found it hard to cope with his illness, but he could not fathom the reason for it. Instead of chatting and joking like they had always done, Chris would prefer to wander off and find something else to do; watching children's cartoons seemed to be his favoured choice. He would sit there for the entire time through the visiting hours and not say a word to anyone.

To Chris, it had only been a few weeks ago that they were playing football in the field together. Everything that he knew had changed in the matter of a day. It had changed for everyone, but Chris was having a harder time accepting it.

"Why won't Chris talk to me, Mum?" James asked as he watched his brother walk away yet again.

"He will soon, love. He's just finding it hard to see you like this, James. Give him time."

James looked across the ward and watched his brother from a distance as he sat in-between the other children. He was not paying attention to the Disney video and there was a blank expression on his face as he ignored the telly and glared at the wall, the normally jolly face that would often have James in stitches now scowling ferociously. James felt illogically guilty that his brother was feeling like this; he felt sorry for him. He knew that he would probably be feeling exactly the same if things had been different and it was Chris that had had the brain tumour.

He knew there was no way that he could have changed anything that had happened but he somehow felt responsible, even though a part of him knew this was an irrational thought. In a way, he thought, it was harder on Chris than it was on himself.

James knew what his own body was capable of and he also knew that it was down to him to work hard and get himself back to normal but all Chris could do was be a spectator and watch as his brother struggled with the things that not long ago had been no problem at all. It was easier for Chris to block it out rather than keep questioning it. He did not like what he was witnessing. James was still his brother and he loved him, but he did not like what was happening to him and discussing his feelings was never a thing that he was comfortable with. Chris always had his own ways of dealing with things and this was just another one of those ways. In his own time he would come to terms with things and James knew that he would be there for him in his own way.

Visiting time was over. It always went too fast for James. He wanted his family there all the time. As Chris pulled his coat from the end of the bed, James tried to talk to him, but words escaped him. How could he not find the words to speak to his own brother – the person he loved, the person who knew him better than anybody else?

After staring deeply into each other's eyes for a few moments, James could see the pain in his brother's eyes for the first time. He saw the fear, doubt, and helplessness etched across his face caused by the gravity of a situation that he just could not handle.

"Chris, it's okay. I'm going to be fine," James whispered, the words forming slowly.

Chris gave a weak smile, but still he did not speak and his smile disappeared as quickly as it took him to slip on his coat. He tried to answer his brother but he had nothing to say, nothing at all. Chris started to walk away, his focus on nothing but the exit. He stopped and looked back at James.

"How do you know?" he asked as tears fell like big, fat raindrops down his cheeks.

"I just do, Chris. I know *everything*, remember?" James replied, with a twinkle in his eye and a reassuring grin.

For the first time, Chris began to smile properly.

Wiping his tears on his sleeve, he sniffed and replied quietly, "Oh yeah, I forgot about that."

James returned the smile. An unspoken conversation and a mutual understanding passed silently between them, something they could not explain, but instinctively accepted.

***

As the days passed, James started to get bored. He was becoming bored of the day-to-day routines and fed up with the endless physical probes and bored of the daily visits from the hospital chaplain.

"Is he coming, Mum?" he asked.

"In about two minutes," his mum replied.

"Tell him I'm asleep," he pleaded, as he yanked the bed covers over his head.

"I can't, James. You've done that too many times and he's going to know that you're not really asleep," she said out of the corner of her mouth as the chaplain moved ever closer.

The chaplain was actually a nice man. His heart was in the right place but his deep Scottish accent grated on James's ears. He no longer wanted to hear his views on life nor his optimistic encouragement being delivered through his wiry, grey beard which was the only thing that remotely disguised his stale, fishy breath.

"Okay, James, he's here. Keep quiet," his mum whispered.

The chaplain walked slowly and passed the end of James's bed.

He turned to James's mum and spoke the words of a man who was in the know: "Asleep again, is he, Mrs Squires? I'm beginning to think that James is avoiding me!"

He smiled and winked and moved on. He must have seen it a hundred times. James's plan had been foiled and he started to feel bad about the whole thing. He did not want to hurt the chaplain's feelings but on the other hand he could not sit through another boring sermon. When the coast was clear, his mum tapped twice on the blanket that was still camouflaging him – a secret tap that had developed naturally over the weeks. Two taps meant the coast was clear; one tap meant that James should stay down; three taps meant that she was not happy with the tap system.

But James did not acknowledge the two taps. His mum pulled his bed covers back gently and smiled to herself when she saw that he had actually fallen asleep for real. He snored quietly and moved his one knee down from his chest, his body now in the position as if he could have been running. His mum thought to herself that he might be dreaming; dreaming of playing football, dreaming of scoring that winning goal. She knew, though, that this would be something he might not ever be able to do again, and her smile turned upside down and she began to cry. She remembered all those football games, all those rugby tournaments, and all those hot days that she and her husband had sat trying to look interested through hours and hours of cricket. Every sport that James had played he had excelled at. She knew that, through everything that had happened, this would be the one thing that James would probably find the hardest to deal with. All they could do was be there for him.

That afternoon, James was feeling in a mischievous mood. He needed to do something to make the days go quicker, something that would bring a smile to his face. Whilst sitting on the toilet, with his mum at the ready just in case he struggled to do the necessary functions that follow a trip to the bathroom, he had a thought. He sat there, his body full of the daily pills that helped to ease the pain and which probably influenced his rash decision to say the following to his mother; things that no child should ever say to his or her mother, words that are best kept within the confines and safety of a playground and well away from any adult. With his mum leaning against the door, her back pushing into the white tiled corner, with one hand resting upon the sink, James began to chat to his mum.

"Mum, can I tell you a joke?"

"Yes, of course."

She had heard many of his jokes over the years and thought nothing of it.

"Are you sure, Mum?" he prompted.

She twigged that this might not be his normal kind of joke but, still humouring him, she replied, "Yes, I'm sure. Is it rude?"

"Err... not really, Mum, no," he replied, not quite meeting her eye. "A postman is walking towards a rather large house. In his hand he has a huge parcel and on getting to the front door he realizes that there is no way it's going to fit through the letterbox." James stopped and looked up at her saying, "See, it's not rude."

His mum was a little relieved as she had imagined the worst at first, but so far so good.

"Carry on," she encouraged.

"Okay," he answered, his voice starting to slur as tiredness started to take over again. "On getting to the front door, the postman could see that the parcel wasn't going to fit through the letterbox so he knocks on the door. A minute passed and nobody answered, so he knocks again. Almost straight away a young boy, aged about eight, opens the door. In one hand he's holding a bottle of Budweiser and in the other he's holding a cigarette." James stretched out his arms, his hands mimicking the grip of a bottle and a cigarette, and he then carried on with his joke. "The postman thinks to himself that this is a little strange and asks the young boy, 'Is your mummy or daddy in?'... Drum roll please... 'Does it bloody look like it?' replies the boy!"

James started to laugh out loud. His mum started to laugh, too, when she watched him. His uncoordinated hands missed each other as he tried to clap, his toes propping up his feet and twisting into the ground as his heels bounced up and down on the brown, tiled floor. Although she was not entirely happy with the swearing, something that in any other situation James would have been in a lot of trouble for, she could see that this was his way of dealing with things. James had always had a great sense of humour, so why should being in hospital change him? This was the thing that would help get him through this, along with his strength and determination. But James did not stop there.

"Mum?" he said.

"What?" his mum asked.

"Who invented the vagina?"

"I don't know, James. Who invented the vagina?" she sighed.

With a smile on his face and cheekiness in his voice he replied, "The county council."

"Go on... Why the county council?" she asked cautiously.

She was curious to know the answer, but she thought she would probably not want to hear it from her son, of all people.

James quickly started with the punch line, "Who else would put a sh—"

His mum hastily cut the joke dead, her words spoken through a smile that only a reprimanding parent could give their recalcitrant child: a smile that clearly said, "*Stop right now, or else.*"

"Okay, James, I think that's enough for today. I think I can guess the rest," she said as sternly as she could.

"Oh, but–" he pleaded.

"Maybe tell me later, eh?"

***

James's stitches had just been removed. It was an event that caused more pain for his dad who was looking on. The stitches were being cut away one at a time, with every movement tugging at his fragile skin as dried up blood flaked away and floated to the floor. A scar was gradually being unveiled; a scar that lay in-between the tiny holes that would be left behind, only to fade away over the years.

His parents had been informed that he would probably be allowed to go home in the next few days, maybe even today. James was thrilled. It had been five long weeks and he was ready to leave the confines of the hospital and get back to his normal life. He was ready to see his friends and ready to sleep in his own bed. There were a few things that needed to be checked first but Mr Dockly was happy with his progress – enough to grant him an early release.

Later on that morning he could hear his parents talking in depth with Mr Dockly. Although he did not understand every word, like 'increased intracranial pressure', he understood the words 'needle', 'spine', and 'fluid'. He had too much liquid building up in his brain and this was causing pressure. James could actually feel this fluid bulging out at the back of his head. It caused a squishy bump right at the top of his new scar, in-between where a part of his skull had been taken away and a dissolvable sponge now taking its place. He compared the pocket of fluid to a pair of Reebok pump trainers; the trainers that he had seen so many times on telly, trainers that he used to want but not anymore!

James was made to lie down on his side, his view fixed deeply into his dad's eyes. He was about to undergo a lumber puncture procedure. His dad kept his full attention, the idea being to keep his son from seeing

73

the large needle that was about to be pushed deep into his spine to extract the unwanted fluid. With his knees drawn up to his chin as far as he could, James felt something being driven into his back. He could not see the needle but it felt infinitely long. He was getting more uncomfortable by the second and his eyes filled with tears of pain. His grip tightened on his dad's hand. His dad tried to keep his face expressionless and James's knuckles turned white as his mum stood watching each and every movement with overwhelming sympathy. She wished that she could take away the pain and that she could be the one to go through all of this instead of her son and that made her feel helpless being unable to do so.

James was lying there as still as he could for over 20 minutes. He felt a fleeting pain run up his leg where the needle had touched a floating nerve and his body started to shake uncontrollably but the movement just caused even more agony. He began to wince and his mum moved towards the bed.

She placed one hand on her husband's shoulder and squeezed it while her other hand lovingly caressed James's face as she said, "Hey, James. Why must it have been the county council who invent the vagina?"

James looked up at his mum quizzically, but his frown soon cleared when he remembered his joke from a previous day. It dawned on him that his mum must have done some research of her own and she knew the punch line now, but she was giving him permission to say it. He took a big breath and delivered the rude punch line with a big grin, forgetting the needle and relieving his discomfort if only for a few moments. James's dad looked up at his wife, his hands still firmly entwined with his son's.

He mouthed the word, "What?" with a confused look on his face, not being in on the joke.

The nurses looked on, stifling their giggles.

As the needle was pulled out slowly, James started to turn his head. He wanted to see the needle; he needed to know what it was that had just been placed in his spine. He first noticed a large thin tube (a manometer, as he later found out) and then he saw it. He did not say a word. He marvelled to himself at how tough he had just been, but that was it. Over the next two hours the nurses regularly checked his spine for any leakage or swelling and he had to lie still on his stomach. Lying still was a skill that James had become very good at over the last few weeks. All he had to do now was wait for the all-clear in order to be allowed to finally go home.

"James, we can go home!" his mum said with a big grin.

As James was about to reply, he felt a jet of warm liquid splatter against his forehead. It streamed down his face and he tasted the water as it dripped into his mouth. He looked around the ward curiously. His investigation started at the bed next to him and swept through the ward until he stopped. His eyes swept back again and there in the bed opposite was the boy called Mark. Armed with a syringe full of water, he was not sure whether to laugh or be worried. The needleless syringe was still in his hand, identifying him as the undeniable culprit. This was unchartered territory: a water fight in the middle of a children's ward? Surely not!

"*Oh yes,*" James thought to himself, "*Let the games begin!*"

"Nurse!" he shouted to the best of his ability. "Can you get me a syringe like Mark's got, please?" he begged, but then he realized he did not need to as it was the nurses' idea, something that they had done many times in the past, and she had already casually placed three big syringes next to his bed.

"Mum, can you fill these up, please?" he asked.

With all three filled to the brim, James was ready for battle. He opted for the biggest one first and prepared to take aim. He tried to push down hard on the plunger, struggling to get a good grip. His hands fumbled and his weapon slipped away through his fingers onto the bed. His mind was focused but his body was failing. He was a gear of war, but the gears were jammed. He pulled the syringe back and tried again. His target was not going anywhere; he just needed to focus. At last the plunger started to go down nicely with the water being released in the right direction. James's hands took control again but the water took a mind of its own. He was still pushing hard, but his objective was about to accidentally change. The water had indeed found a target, but, unfortunately, it was the wrong target. The chaplain shot up out of the chair that was placed next to another patient's bed nearby. Cold water trickled down the nape of the chaplain's neck and down into his collar.

"Was that really necessary, James?" he called out crossly, taking off his jacket.

James's mum began to chuckle, her mirth increasing when the chaplain asked her if she thought her son's actions were acceptable. The chaplain almost huffed like a child and advertised his disappointment clearly whilst charging out of the ward, his words of discontent being heard by everyone.

James began to get to grips with his intent: Mark was still his mark. Using the slightly smaller syringe, he fired. The water flew through the air with conviction and gravity played its part well as it doused Mark's ALF endorsed pyjamas. The floor was soaked and the nurses tried to mop it, but they just could not keep up with the consequences of battle. One nurse almost slipped over, only to be saved by a colleague – she had almost become a statistic, a casualty of war. The children were ecstatic as the nurses threw themselves, quite literally, into the game.

"Okay, lads! Sister's coming with Mr Dockly. Let's put the game to bed, shall we?" a nurse said in a panic suddenly.

James yielded his weapons with good grace, but Mark, however, very naughtily kept hold of one of his. Mr Dockly approached James's bed. He was allowed to go as soon as he was ready. He had forgotten all about the fun that had just happened. Anybody could have offered him a million water fights but going home was all he wanted to do. In a routine glance around the ward, a silent communication to let everyone know that his days in the hospital were over, he espied Mark. He was filling up his syringe from beneath his covers, and then he raised his right hand and with his thumb he expertly depressed the plunger. A tiny drop of orange liquid jumped into the air and landed on James's white pillowcase, leaving a tell-tale stain which spread and grew bigger on contact. James could do nothing as he watched silently. Another surge of orange juice soared through the air. It grew nearer and then dipped as it daringly reached Mark's intended victim. His screams of delight and his yelps of accomplishment abruptly stopped and his look turned to one of terror, with the recognition of his actions quickly setting in. Mr Dockly removed a handkerchief from his pocket and wiped his face, the juice leaving a sticky residue on his Ralph Lauren shirt. He smiled patronizingly at Mark and then turned to the Sister.

"We've had words about this before, haven't we, Sister?"

"Yes, Mr Dockly. I'm sorry, I don't know how he got hold of the syringe," she replied demurely.

As Mr Dockly began to walk away Sister followed him and then looked back at the other nurses, giving them a droll look. The nurses one by one began to smile; they did not envy the chat that was about to take place between Mr Dockly and Sister. They knew, however, that Sister did not mind their shenanigans one little bit. She and her staff would do anything to make life just that little bit better for the children in their charge.

When James woke up that night, he found himself confused as to where he was. There was no crying, the temperature seemed just right, and he was being left alone to sleep. The gap in the door allowed him to see the dog lying upside down in her basket; her dreams of running activated by her legs sleepwalking through the air. The sound of the grandmother clock striking one also added comfort to his sleep and he snuggled back down. James was happy to be home.

When James woke up the following morning, the first thing he heard was the deep drawn snoring emanating from his brother' bed. Next he could smell the toast wafting up the stairs and into his bedroom, rousing him further. His family was up early – well, apart from Chris, of course. Although this was not the normal Saturday morning that James was used to, at least the surroundings were familiar and comforting.

"Breakfast is ready," his mother said as she walked through the door and went to help James up from his bed.

"Christopher, wake up! Your breakfast is ready!" she shouted across the room, his movements gradually being noticed from beneath the duvet.

"Why have you done breakfast, Mum? You never do breakfast on a Saturday morning. Can't I have mine later?" Chris grumbled.

"Everybody's up, Chris. Can you just get up, please."

Tiredly and grumpily, Chris managed to drag himself out of bed. His feet seemed almost too heavy as he shuffled them over the carpet towards the bathroom.

"It's too early to be getting up, Mum," Chris moaned.

"It's 10.30, Chris. Stop moaning," replied their mother.

"Yeah, exactly! Too early... Okay, okay! Don't worry, I'm getting up!"

Everybody chatted and laughed at the breakfast table. The dog waited patiently for any scrap of food that might 'accidentally on purpose' fall from the table. Their dad was taking yet another day off work to be a part of James's first morning home. This was something that made James appreciate the people in his life, and small things like breakfast that could mean so much to him.

It did not take long for Chris to wake up properly and be alert to all the food that was now placed before him, not finishing his toast before he started on his eggs. Oh, how he liked his food!

"Leave some for other people, Chris. It's not all for you," Collette said irritably.

"I'm tired, Coll, and that makes me hungry – you know that," he replied, filling his mouth with yet more scrambled egg. "Anyway, you're always on a diet, so I can have your share, can't I?"

"That's enough, please, Christopher," their mum said sternly, swiftly trying to defuse a possible argument.

"Well, it's true," James remarked casually.

Everything went quiet. Even the dog did not dare breathe. Chris turned and smiled at James and together they both looked at their sister. Everybody was looking at her, each person imagining what her reaction might be. Judging by the look on her face, she must have thought about getting angry at first, but that expression turned to a smile and that smile developed into a chuckle. Everything was still the same, but different. Everyone now had the reasoning to put things into perspective, even if it did not last forever. The little squabbles just did not seem that important anymore. Fractious tempers thwarted, the rest of breakfast was enjoyed by all and even the dog was rewarded with a share of the bacon. (Accidentally-on-purpose, of course!)

It was a few months before James was up to his old tricks again and Chris was to be his first victim. Chris was a strong believer in the paranormal; particularly aliens and anything else that he could not explain. He was also a very deep sleeper, just like their sister. The house could blow up and Chris would still be snuggled under the warmth of his duvet, snoring and smiling at whatever weird and wonderful dream he might be having.

James watched Chris getting ready for bed one night and patiently waited until he had drifted off to sleep. Quietly making his way through and over the clothes that covered the floor, nearly tripping over a pair of muddy football boots that were hidden underneath a pair of unwashed rugby shorts, James's latest prank began to take shape. Leaning over the bed, he gently touched Chris's shoulder – no response. He pushed a little bit harder then stood back, waiting for some sort of reaction – not a peep. James was ready to begin.

Gently pulling back the covers to reveal Chris's feet, James momentarily covered his nose when the cheesy smell hit his senses hard. It was so bad that he almost considered aborting the whole operation. Holding his breath and remembering the time that Chris's feet had caused him and two friends to leave him to sleep alone in a tent whilst camping because the smell was so unbearable, James bravely continued. Finding a dirty, odd sock on the floor, James started slowly to pull it onto Chris's foot. This was a practical joke that was going to work over a matter of weeks, maybe even months. James was willing to play the long, waiting game.

After the first stage was complete, James made his way back to his own bed. As he took the first few quiet steps back he stopped and lifted one foot off the floor, the result of forgetting about the football boot and stepping on the worn plastic and sharpened studs. James limped back and slowly got into his own bed.

"It's time to get up, Chris. You'll be late for school," their mum shouted the next morning.

Five minutes passed and Chris was shouted at again, this time a little bit louder. He started to stir and James peeked from beneath his covers and watched to see if he would notice the sock. With growing anticipation he watched Chris sit up on the side of his bed and rub his eyes and then look down but he did not bat an eyelid at the fact that he was already wearing one sock as he stretched his arm out and retrieved another dirty sock. They weren't even matching, but he gave it a quick sniff and then slipped it over his foot. James was a little disappointed but his next words would help plant the seeds for things that were yet to come.

"Chris, did you feel something in the room last night?" James asked nonchalantly.

"Like what?" Chris replied.

"I'm not sure. I just felt a cold breeze early this morning."

"No, never felt a thing. Maybe we've got a ghost," he said jokingly.

"Don't be stupid, Chris. There's no such thing," James said, trying to hold back a smile, knowing that the idea would be taking root in his brother's mind now.

James left it at that for a couple of weeks before starting on the second part of his prank. He again waited for Chris to fall asleep and then tiptoed across to the other side of the bedroom. He skipped the gentle touch and pushed down on Chris's shoulder.

Chris started to move and then he suddenly said, "Don't worry, Superman's here. I will fly and catch the fish."

James panicked a little at first but then had to stop himself from laughing when he realized that Chris was sleep talking. Preparing himself this time for the smell, James pulled up the covers from his brother's feet. He had to rethink the plan quickly when he saw that Chris was already wearing a pair of socks. There was only one thing for it. With his mum and dad still downstairs watching telly, James made his way past the living room and into the kitchen.

"Just getting a drink of water, Mum," he called out as he passed the living room door.

"Okay, then straight back to bed, please. You've got your first day back at school tomorrow, don't forget."

James had not forgotten this fact. He was nervous about it, of course. It was going to be only for half a day to start with but he was not looking forward to the looks or the questions that he knew he was going to get. Putting it to the back of his mind he continued to the kitchen but instead of getting himself some water he began to rummage through the contents of the tumble dryer. After a few seconds of searching and then grabbing the items that he needed, he made his way back upstairs.

Chris's feet were still uncovered so James finished the deed as quickly as he could and, now being tired himself, got into bed and almost as soon as his head touched the pillow he was fast asleep.

"James, wake up!" Chris called out as he nudged him awake.

Opening his eyes slowly, he turned to see his brother crouching over him.

"You know you mentioned that you felt something in the room the other night?"

It took a few seconds for James to realize that his joke was now in full swing.

"Yeah, why?" he replied, managing to keep a straight face.

"Did you feel anything last night?" Chris said with a puzzled look on his face.

"No, why?" James replied, still maintaining a straight face.

"Because I woke up this morning with a pair of pink socks on, that's why!"

"What *are* you on about?" James asked, feigning confusion.

"When I went to bed last night I'm sure I was wearing *my* socks but when I woke up just now I had *these* on my feet!" he said, placing one foot on the side of James's bed and pointing at the offending pink sock.

"Chris, I don't know what you're talking about. Let me sleep," James said as he rolled over to hide a smirk.

"You're at school today, so get up," Chris said as he turned and looked down at his feet, questioning himself one last time.

He then bent over and picked up the dirty socks that James had taken off him and put them on over the pink ones.

***

"Morning, James. How are you feeling?" James's form teacher asked him as he sat down at his desk.

"I'm okay, thank you."

There was not anything else that he wanted to say. He just wanted things to get back to normal and be treated the same as everyone else. After that initial meeting James realized that he did not need to feel nervous; there was no staring or sympathetic looks. Of course, there was the odd question here and there, but, overall, things seemed to get back to normal very quickly.

This was helped by Paddy. Paddy was a big, rugby-playing, Irish lout. He was more concerned with how his short, blond hair looked than being nice to people. That afternoon, in an English lesson, everybody was sitting casually in the library discussing the topic that Miss McQueen had just handed them. Paddy sat down, placing his right foot underneath his bottom, and relaxed. He was never one for an intelligent conversation. Instead, he preferred to just make fun of the people around him.

The chatter went on for most of the hour. By this time everyone, including James, was fed up with Paddy's immature comments. He sat there and twiddled his thumbs, crunching his knuckles with his shovel-like hands, making inane comments, just waiting for the end of the lesson. With the bell ringing twice, class was now over. This was a relief for the ones that did not have Paddy in their next lesson, but not for the ones who did. Everyone began to stand up from the comfy library chairs, pulling their bags out from beneath the table as they did. James watched as Paddy began to pull his foot out from underneath his bottom and place it on the floor. James then saw him stand up and immediately fall to his right and crash down on the hard, wooden floor. At first James was worried, but not for long. Paddy did not appear to have hurt himself during the fall. The only thing that caused him to fall in the first place was the fact that his leg had gone numb because he had sat on it for the past hour. Laughter erupted as everyone watched him lying there. The embarrassment of it all would stay with Paddy a lot longer than the pins and needles in his leg would. Nobody helped him up; nobody even offered. If there was one person who deserved the humiliation of his own stupidity, it was Paddy. James knew that from that point on things would get back to normal.

That night, after a good day at school, James decided to follow up quickly on the pink socks incident. With the timing now well-rehearsed, he crept over to Chris again. He did not bother to check this time if he was fast asleep. Knowing that Chris already thought that there was probably a ghost, or something to that affect, in the room, James executed his plan swiftly and went straight to his own bed and soon fell asleep himself.

"James, wake up!"

"What?"

"I felt something last night," Chris said, his imagination convincing him that there was something unexplainable going on.

He never looked for logic and James knew that this would be the one thing that would help him get the best out of this prolonged joke.

"Like what?" James asked.

"Well, I never heard anything, but I felt a tingling during the night and when I got up I had the pink socks back on and one shoe."

"Chris, you probably forgot to take them off," James suggested.

"No, I didn't… Hang on, are *you* doing this?"

The penny could almost be heard as it nearly dropped but James acted like a pro and it only took a few well thought out words to convince Chris that he had nothing to do with it. Not wanting to push his luck, James decided to leave the joke on standby for a few weeks before beginning again. With each addition to Chris's night-time dressing James added another item or two, leaving a gap of a few weeks in-between each prank.

"James! James, wake up!"

James rolled over and laughed out loud immediately. Chris was standing there in his boxer shorts with his arms outstretched. He was now wearing the pink socks, a pair of odd shoes, knee pads, elbow pads, a scarf, gloves, and a hat. James still did not let on that it was him creeping around during the night.

"James, this had better not be your doing!" Chris said in a panicky voice.

James just shook his head and denied all knowledge.

"Mum!" Chris called out as he knocked on their parents' bedroom door and walked in.

James giggled to himself as he listened to the muffled voices which turned quickly into uncontrollable shrieks of laughter.

At breakfast Chris looked across the table at James and Collette, his mind ticking over as he glared balefully at them both. He had his suspicions that it must have been one of them… *or was it?* James did not want to spoil his joke so he never uttered another word about it, ever.

Chapter 5

1992

The last year and a half had been tough for James. He was obviously a lot stronger, but a few disabilities still remained. One of these was his speech. His words would still come out mumbled and his sentences sometimes came out slurred. This only really happened when he was tired. The shaking, however, was becoming more and more a part of his everyday life. If he found himself in a situation that he was not used to e.g., being the first person in a queue at the shops, or as a passenger on a train full of people who had grabbed all the available seats leaving James nothing else to do but stand, his body would start to jerk, his spine would begin to ache at the base, and his chest would move backwards and forward. This left his head to do nothing else but wobble; wobble like the plastic dogs that lived in the back window of many cars, the toys that became a novelty, something funny for people to chortle at.

James did not want to be a novelty. He conceded, however, that if he had to live in a world of awkwardness then he would be the first to laugh. He made fun of himself at college if a pencil got a life of its own and jumped out of his hand. If he spilled his drink whilst walking across the dinner hall he would say, "Don't mind me, I wasn't that thirsty anyway!" to the people watching and wondering why, when he left the drinks machine, his cup was full and now it was half empty. This life was much better than the one it nearly was: in a wheelchair, or even worse.

James sat at the bar of the Morgan pub. It was full of underage drinkers. It was a venue that welcomed the naivety of its punters, as long as they had cash weighing down the pockets of their fashionable jeans. Paisley shirts staggered around the room bumping into anything that got in their way. There were patched denims to be seen whichever way James looked and dungarees only being kept up with one buckle, all moving around in time to the rocking tunes of Oasis and Blur.

"Pint of Diesel, please," James said.

"How old are you?" the barman questioned.

He paused for a split second but then managed to say, "Eighteen," just before his body started to shake.

"Date of birth?"

Another question and another reason for James to panic. He was sure his shaking would give him away.

"15th of August 1973," James replied with slight confidence.

The barman started to pour the drink. That was all he needed – no ID and no arguments. First went in the cider, then the lager mixed in, and then a dash of blackcurrant. James searched his pockets for coins and handed over the £1.80 in twenty pence pieces and two fifties. He felt good. He felt like a man as he walked away from the bar. He took a big gulp from his drink, a swig to lessen the amount of beer in his glass: the less there was in the glass, the less there was to spill. Leaning coolly against the cigarette-stained wall, James noticed a girl sitting talking to her friends in the corner.

"Tony, who's that?" he asked.

"Who?" Tony replied, trying to see which direction that James was looking.

"Her, with the short, brown hair and dark, brown eyes."

"Oh, that's Vicky, mate. Well out of your league, son."

Tony was only a few months older than James, but he always ended his remarks with 'son'. This annoyed James sometimes but tonight he only had one thing on his mind: Vicky.

"I'm going over; wish me luck," James boasted hopefully, the drink now flowing.

"This is going to be funny. Hey, lads, come here. James is going to try and pull Vicky Reynolds," Tony called out to his mates.

With Pearl Jam's '*Alive*' blaring in the background, James walked over, taking a large swig of Dutch courage en route, with the chorus reaching its climax just as he started to speak.

"Hi," he said.

Vicky looked James up and down but her eyes made no contact with his whatsoever. She looked back at her friends and sparked up another conversation with them, ignoring him totally. James turned around, his confidence crushed, and the only thing stopping him from shaking was the Diesel. The alcohol actually helped James's condition. He never realized that drinking could actually be good for him! He took another large swig and then looked over at his friends, all of whom were spilling their own drinks with laughter and delighting in James's crash and burn.

Tony made the actions of a plane and shouted, "Mayday! Mayday!"

James stopped in-between two tables. He turned and placed his nearly empty pint on the one in front of two Goths. He then looked at Tony with a smile that oozed confidence, with body language to match, and he walked straight back to Vicky.

"Hi, I'm James. Can I get you a drink?" he said with impressive assertiveness.

"Yeah sure, James. Sit down a minute first," she replied, offering him a stool.

Tony and the rest of the gang watched in amazement. They could not believe what they were witnessing. Nobody in their year had ever got this close to Vicky, let alone sat next to her to chat. James had gone from a normal boy to a god in the space of two minutes. After a while and well into the jokes and banter, James brought up his offer of a drink again. He walked passed his mates with verve. His wink caused envy with his peers, but he did not care and he swayed on by to the bar.

"Pint of Diesel, and a vodka and coke, please."

He was much more assertive the second time around.

"How old are you?" came the response.

"W-what?" James asked nervously.

"What age are you? Simple question!"

"Erm... 18. I just had a drink from you, not five minutes ago."

"I know you did, but you said that you were born in 1973; that would make you 19, not 18."

James had nothing to say. No comeback, and his swagger was no more.

"That makes you *too old* to drink, my friend. Now get out of here – you're barred!" the barman shouted just as the music began to fade.

Everyone heard his rise and fall from boy to god and back to boy again. James did not know what to do. His friends had disappeared to avoid any chance of them getting kicked out as well. He walked away and out through the back door. There was no way that he was going to let Vicky see him like this. Hopefully he would never have to see her again, at all. As he made his quick getaway, with his head down, he accidentally bumped into an incoming punter. Saying sorry, he tried to move around him.

"Squires! What are you doing here?"

James looked up when he recognized the voice of Daniel, who was standing in the doorway.

"Nothing, now. I'm going home."

He again tried to walk away, only to be stopped by Daniel's next comment.

"Yeah, run along, Shaky. It's well past your bedtime, you freak! Oh, by the way – stay away from Vicky, she's mine and she don't like *retards!*"

The venom in his voice matched the rage on his face. James turned back. He knew that what he was about to say would result in a good kicking, but he could not help himself.

"Oh, yeah?" he said, as he raised his head from looking at Daniel's shoes and steadily met his hostile eyes.

"Vicky asked me to pass on a message. She said you're an idiot and she doesn't want to see you anymore."

Without hesitation, Daniel grabbed him by the scruff of the neck and, with James's toes being the only thing touching the ground, Daniel drew back his right fist. Out of nowhere came someone else's hand from behind James and gripped tightly around Daniel's poised knuckles.

"It's all right, bro'. I've got this."

Chris stepped angrily in front of Daniel, lowering Daniel's arm as he did so. Without warning, Chris punched him hard on the nose with a right jab. Daniel lost his balance and stumbled backwards. Chris then swung hard with his left fist making contact with his jaw, creating a cracking sound. Daniel was still managing to stand, blood pouring from his nostrils. Chris moved in again, this time with a right hook smashing against the side of Daniel's cheek. Daniel swivelled to his right and his legs twisted around each other as he spun to the ground, hitting it like a sack of spuds. Chris turned calmly to his brother and blew a sigh of relief.

"That could have gone completely the wrong way," he said as he tapped James on the shoulder and walked into the pub.

James did not know that his brother had it in him. He had never seen him lose his temper like that before. It seemed as though he had just released a year and a half of built up anger with Daniel being there to help him release it. It was his way of making amends for not being able to do anything the day that James was thrown across the park and the months that followed; his way of bringing his own trauma to an end. James walked away with a feeling of pride, replaying his brother's boxing prowess in his mind. He shoved his hands deep into his pockets and began the long walk home, with his head dipped down to the ground as he kicked a stone into the road.

"James, wait," a soft voice called from behind him.

When he turned around he saw Vicky walking towards him.

"Can you walk me home, James? I don't live that far from you," she requested.

They walked the two miles together. It was as if their earlier conversation had not finished. The words never stopped and there were no awkward silences.

After that night, James and Vicky saw a great deal of each other. They met after college most nights and on weekends they spent most of the time kissing or doing something they should not have been doing. A few months went by and James got to know Vicky very well indeed. Not as well as any teenage boy would like, but well enough. He had the upmost respect for Vicky and women in general; something that came naturally, helped over the years by his good upbringing.

One afternoon, James and Vicky decided to take a shortcut home. This shortcut would take them through the grounds of Malvern Girls' School and over the common, a field that was currently overgrown with bracken. Each step James took was full of anticipation. His heart began to race and his palms were clammy. Was this what he thought it was going to be? Sure, he had imagined this moment over and over in his head but in reality he had no idea what he was doing.

Vicky found a secluded spot. The sun did its job as it beat down hard on them both. She then decided that the way forward was to take her jumper off, using the heat as an excuse as she sexily slid it up her body and over her head. James tried not to ogle: his eyes would have popped out if that had been physically possible. He was one step ahead of her already in his head and he had already got to the bra stage well before she had.

But James then panicked. He had never taken off a girl's bra before. He could not even remember ever touching one. He had heard all the locker room jokes, the talk that most teenage boys have at some point in their lives. What if he could not unclip it? What if it was a front fastener and he did not realize? This was all too much; then a second dread started to set in. This was the field that he had walked across many times. He suddenly remembered the morning, afternoon, and evening strolls with his father, with the dog bounding over the grass and into the fresh water that flowed just yards away.

"We can't do this here, Vic. My dad walks the dog on this common."

"It's fine, James, nobody can see us," she replied, pulling him towards the ground as she lay back.

"No, I mean he's off work today. He could turn up at any minute."

"Stop worrying, we will just have to be quiet. Anyway, his car wasn't there, was it?"

"True," he answered, but still in doubt as to whether this was a good idea.

Vicky had now got down to her black, lacy bra. He didn't care now. His hesitation melted away – nothing would stop them now. He was doing remarkably well, considering five minutes ago he was a novice. His jeans were now around his ankles and his t-shirt decorated the bracken along with Vicky's bra. This was it: this was his first time… This was a triumph!

"Can you hear something, Vicky?"

"Seriously, James, stop it. You're ruining the moment," she moaned.

James listened out carefully but never heard another thing so he quickly found his rhythm and started again where he had left off.

"Did you hear that, James?"

"Seriously, Vicky, you're ruining the moment!" he laughed.

"No, I think someone's coming."

"Hopefully, yeah!" he jested.

Vicky stopped. Using both hands she pushed James away, her face indicating something that he did not want to see. He reluctantly lifted his head up towards the gap in the bracken that he and Vicky had engineered. He was met with an almost cinematic cliché: eight strangers' smiling faces beamed down on his bare backside, their heads creating a perfect circle. This was the place where the Territorial Army would often do their training exercises. James remained motionless for a moment with his elbows nestled in the grass, then covered his drooping head with his hands.

Things got worse. Vicky grabbed her clothing and escorted herself away from the situation quickly. This left James to face the army on his own. He turned to his audience and started to explain, not really knowing what he was going to say.

"Okay, I know this is—" He stopped midsentence. "Bess, what are you doing here?"

James's dog had seen all the commotion and decided to take a look. If the dog was here then his dad would not be far behind...

"And the day started so well," he groaned under his breath.

With precision and well-practised manoeuvres, the TA lads aided his escape. With a pair of borrowed combat trousers that were two sizes too big and a commandeered rucksack, they made their move. James jogged alongside his newly-found friends with trepidation, seeking out his father over the bobbing berets. He could not see him anywhere; maybe he had gone. He was not so lucky. Just ahead and emerging from a well-hidden embankment, James caught a glimpse of his dad's cap-covered head.

"About turn!" James shouted, disguising his voice.

To his amazement it worked: the squadron moved 180 degrees to the right as his dad watched them. He admired the discipline and time that had gone into their work. He moved back slightly in order to make way for the few that threatened to brush him on their way past. They had never left a man behind and they were not about to start now. James kept his head down and kept up the pace. They all carried on to the gate and beyond, leading their comrade to safety.

That evening James walked into his house with self-assurance. He knew that his dad had not seen anything; everything was normal. Throwing his jumper over the dining room chair, he made his way to the kitchen. His mum and dad relaxed in the living room as he searched for something to eat. Grabbing a packet of crisps and a Club bar from the fridge, he made his way to his bedroom. He greeted his parents briefly as he passed the living room door quickly.

"About turn!" called his dad, his face still behind his newspaper.

James stopped suddenly. His eyes widened and his mouth fell open, with the half-chewed chocolate bar sitting precariously on his lips. James pretended at first not to hear him but the realization of his dad's remark had hit home immediately.

"Come on, son, quick march!" his father followed up.

James leaned against the doorframe. He had no army to help him out of this one.

"Um... yeah, Dad?" he asked, his voice slightly quieter than normal.

"Good day today, son?"

"Not bad. Why?"

"Just asking, that's all."

His dad folded up the paper and inspected his son's reaction. His questioning hit all the right buttons, leaving James nothing else to do but squirm.

"Can I go now, Dad?" he asked, already halfway to getting away.

"Of course you can, James. Just don't forget to return those army trousers," his mum said from behind the wall, both his parents giggling to themselves as James ran up the stairs feeling distraught.

James did not see much of Vicky after that day. One day he saw her walking happily into town hand in hand with one of the squaddies. He had obviously seen something he liked.

Chapter 6

"Chris, there's a strange lad at the front door for you. He's either been let out on day release or he's escaped from somewhere," their dad announced early one sunny Saturday morning.

Chris knew straight away to whom his dad was referring as he hesitantly made his way to the front door in embarrassment to greet his badly-timed and unwanted visitor.

Max was a strange lad. Strange in personality as well as in appearance, he always wore jeans that were always almost a couple of inches too short. This was made even more noticeable due to his odd choice of wearing bright, white socks with black, slip-on shoes. It was a well-known fact that he was a massive Michael Jackson fan so maybe that was why his clothes sense was always a little bit weird. Chris was just relieved he did not opt to wear a single sequined glove on his right hand and constantly moonwalk.

Opening the front door that his dad had obviously pushed shut to keep the mad boy at bay, Chris approached his friend. Max could never stand still. He would rock from foot to foot and his hands would always be busy doing something. His favourite thing was to make fists and poke his index fingers in and out at opposite times, occasionally adding his thumbs into the digit dance.

His words sounded as though they were being spoken painfully through his large, pointed nose with oversized nostrils to match. His laugh sounded like something straight out of a horror film and his teeth would put the fear of God into any child under the age of eight. Many of his nicknames were the result of his huge buck teeth: Esther, Ken, and Dodd, but Dobbin seemed to be the most popular name of them all. That's what having equine teeth will do. It was often remarked and joked about that Max was possibly the only person in the world who could easily eat an apple through a letterbox!

"You coming out?" Max asked in a nasally tone.

"Yeah, might do. Where are you going?"

"Stu and Scott are going up to the girls' college to see if they can pull one of the French girls that have just started there. Fancy having a go?"

"Yeah all right, mate. Give me two minutes," Chris replied as he turned and walked back into the house.

Max started to follow without any hint of an invite. Chris spun around quickly and placed both his palms on Max's chest.

"I said *give me two minutes*. Actually, mate, I'll meet you at the end of the road."

Although Chris actually quite liked Max he was also well aware that he quite often spoke the words of a maniac. This would only add to the iffy first impression that Max had already given his father. The further away the better, Chris thought. Max must have been used to this kind of reaction as he never even questioned Chris's request and stepped out of the entrance and walked back down the garden path, heading to the end of the road.

"Are you coming out, James?" Chris called out as he sat on the stairs tying his laces.

"Where are you going?"

"Just out. You coming, or what?"

"Yeah, okay, why not."

"Make sure you take that boy back to wherever he came from, lads," their dad shouted from the living room and then began to laugh out loud to himself.

James, Chris, and Max made their way through the alleyways and country lanes, over the common, and into the town centre. A few more roads later and they had reached their destination: Malvern Girls' College. Pointing at a shaking and trembling bush outside one of the main dormitories, Max moved towards it whilst shouting about his discovery.

"Shh!" the bush hissed.

"Hey, James, is it me or did that bush just talk?" joked Chris.

"All right, Scott. Where's Stu?" Max continued.

"I'm here... Be quiet... I think they might know we're hiding."

Scott pointed between his legs at Stu who was lying down flat on his stomach in-between Scott's feet, his eyes on the front door to the main part of the college – the door that he had seen three French girls enter just two days before. Scott was on a mission. A challenge that he had tried many times before but with each attempt resulting in failure – different girls, of course, but this time he had convinced himself that things would turn out differently.

"Chris, can you see anyone in the upstairs window?"

"Which upstairs window? There's loads of 'em!" he exclaimed, moving his eyes along the continuous row of shining glass.

"Any window... Just check them all," replied Stu.

Chris continued to spy each and every window. He stopped scanning the windows only when he finally saw two gorgeous foreign girls peering out the window. The girls were clued up to the events that were about to unfold and were giggling at the impromptu show.

"Hey, Stu, are these two the ones you're on about?" he asked.

"Where? Where?" he called as he tried to drag himself out of the bush. "Get off me!" he shouted, lifting Scott off his feet for a second. "Yep, that's them. Beautiful or what, James, eh?"

"Not bad, but you've got no chance," he replied.

"What do you mean? Because I have, mate. I've just got to turn on the charm, that's all."

"No, I mean you haven't got a chance of meeting them. This place is like Fort Knox; there ain't no way you're getting in there, my friend."

Stu was never one to give up and walk away – run away, maybe, but never walk. His last attempt had resulted in a full-on chase from the deputy head after he had been caught sneaking in through the back door and into the empty (so he thought) kitchen. It had taken all of his local knowledge of the cut-throughs and hiding places for him to be able to escape. This time, however, he was willing to put himself through the whole ordeal again just to get to chat to the French beauties.

"My God, look at them! They are *so* worth it!"

"Yes, they are. But that still doesn't solve the problem of how exactly you're going to get *to* them," stated Max, the first sensible thing anyone had heard him say for a long time. But then he reverted back to form with, "What if I climb up the tree and across to the window?"

With the tree being at least eight feet away from the nearest window, and the wrong window at that, Max was back to his predictable, not-so-bright self.

"Don't be stupid, Max," Chris said.

Stu told him to hush and said, "Great idea, Max. You carry on with that and we'll try to come up with something else." He turned and whispered, "Let's see how long it takes him to realize there's no way *that* plan's gonna work. Anyway, he might give us the distraction we need – I have an idea."

Still hiding behind the bush they huddled together as Max ran off and began his tree ascent. After the plan had been discussed, and with Max now halfway up the oak tree, each one took their position. With all of them now gripping an apple that had just been handpicked from the orchard over the road, the wheels of their under-thought ideas were put into motion.

"You throw yours first, Scott. James, you next. Then Chris, and then me."

The idea was to throw the apples at the front door and, hopefully, when it was answered someone would walk outside and investigate who and why there was nobody there. This would give Stu his vital opportunity to sneak behind them and into the house. He knew that only half the staff would be working on a Saturday; all he needed to do was make it up to the dormitory, and the rest would be history.

"The stuff that legends are made of," he muttered underneath his breath.

This was probably the only thing he ever told himself under his breath as there were many obstacles that he would voluntarily place in front of himself, with this one being one of the more adventurous.

"Hey, lads, what are you doing? I'm nearly there," Max shouted down as he pushed himself along the branch towards the wrong window, trying desperately to keep his balance as his hands gripped and grasped at anything that could to stop him from falling to the ground.

"Max, be quiet and don't move a muscle for a minute. We'll tell you when to make your move," Chris called back.

Scott threw the first apple along the ground and into the large, blue door creating a heavy thud as it made contact with the wood. It must have sounded like someone was trying to kick down the door if you had happened to be on the inside but there was no response. Nobody even came to the door, let alone open it and come outside.

"James, you're up next. Remember: fast and low, fast and low," Stu instructed.

James did exactly what was asked of him and again the apple hit the door with a thundering whack, but there was still no reply to their ambitious attempts at getting the door opened.

"Hey, lads, I've got a bad feeling about this. I can't reach the window but I can see something moving inside!" Max shouted.

His voice sounded more and more worried the further he travelled along the now bending branch as it started to dawn on him just what he had got himself into and not having a clue how he was going to get himself out of it. He still, however, stupidly tried to reach out to the protruding window ledge; a ledge that was nowhere nearer to him no matter how far he stretched out his bruised and scratched arms.

"Seriously, guys, I'm scared now. It's really high up here. Don't throw anymore apples. Wait for me to get back down, please."

His request fell upon deaf ears as Chris released his sweet, aroma-scented ammunition.

"Chris, I said to keep it low!" Stu shouted.

He slowly moved his hands up to his face and attempted to cover his eyes but still watched the apple as it went crashing through the top half of the door... the *glass* half. All five of them stared at the now smashed door. They all turned their heads suddenly upwards at the sound of a screeching window that opened above them; the window that Max was, and had been for a good five minutes, trying to escape from.

"What the *hell* is going on?" screamed the voice of a very angry woman.

"Leg it!" Chris shouted, although they were all thinking it.

"What about Max? We can't just leave him," said James as he, too, started to run.

He turned to see the middle-aged woman and Max staring hard at each other, each one waiting to see who would make the first move. She knew that the only way Max was going to get down was if he had the nerve to jump the 10-foot gap between him and the ground, but she also knew that he was scared. She decided to make her calculated move first and started making her way downstairs quickly.

Max shuffled and shook his body backwards as quickly as he could, then they all heard the sound of a deafening crack. It did not matter how far away they had run, this was a noise that made their hearts almost stop and they knew instantly what the outcome would be. They watched with horror as Max plummeted to the ground with ferocious speed, still gripping the broken branch. His normally tanned face turned white with fear the further he fell and the last thing they all saw was something that would stay in their minds for years to come: white socks and black, slip-on shoes as they disappeared behind a large bush.

As quick as a flash, and with a hint of guilt, Stu came out with the final words of the moment before he continued to run away: "Oh, he's gonna get it *bad*... so let's *beat it!*"

After getting away as far as they could and laughing at each other in-between catching their breath, they all began to feel bad at the thought of what their unlucky friend might now be going through.

"I can't believe we just left him there," James remarked.

"What else were we supposed to do, mate? We would all be in trouble now if we had gone back and, anyway, it's only Max," Scott replied.

Chris retorted, "What do you mean it's *only* Max? He's still a mate!"

He was clearly quite angry at Scott's thoughtless comment.

"You know what I mean. It's only Dobbin. Who would you rather it was instead, then – you?"

Chris went quiet and just glared at his increasingly annoying friend.

"Nah, didn't think so. Let's just go," Scott replied smugly.

They all moved on and made sure to walk the long way back, through the park and past the old bandstand that stood in the middle of it and had become a general meeting place over the years for many a teenager. They suddenly heard the deep witchlike cackle that could only be Max. If the laugh did not convince them of his presence then it was sure to be the sight of the toddler crying and running back to his parents who had been having a relaxing picnic but were now trying to convince their child that monsters do not exist.

"Hello, fellas. Where have you been?" Max said cheerfully as he leaned casually, and almost triumphantly, on one of the bandstand posts.

"Max! What happened?" James asked.

Max described his great escape, obviously exaggerating wherever possible to enhance his tale that would be told again and again from now on. It had turned out that when the branch had snapped, and after they had watched him fall to his apparent doom, he had been saved by his now muddy and torn sport socks. Behind the bush, where they could not see events unfold, in the last few feet of his plummet the cuff of his sock had got caught in one of the last small, but perfectly sized, branches. It was not enough, however, to stop him completely but just enough to slow him down and get him into a great starting off position to make his sprint away.

They all listened with admiration right until the end, but what they did not expect was for Max to also gain the names of all three of the French girls when they had thrown a piece of paper out the window and in the path of his miraculous escape. The five of them made their way home marvelling at the amazing adventures that none of them could have dreamed of when they had woken up that morning. Max received a pat on the back from each and every one of his friends as they all strolled through the park. They did not want the fun to end quite just yet.

"What are we doing later, lads?" Max asked with excitement.

"Dunno, mate. Fancy going into Worcester?" Chris replied.

They all decided to meet up outside the newsagent. This was always the best place to meet up because the bus stop was ideally situated directly outside and also it gave them all the chance to stock up on sweets and drinks for their short bus journey into Worcester.

"Has anyone seen Ken? Is he not coming, then?" James asked.

"Who the hell's Ken?" laughed Scott.

"Ken Dodd. Ya know – Max. You not heard that one before?" Stu answered.

"Oh yeah, of course I have. I just forgot. He's got so many names that it's hard to keep up."

"Honestly, Scott, there's not a lot up there, is there?" Stu said as he jokingly tapped Scott's forehead with his knuckles.

"Here he comes. Oh my God, what the hell has he got with him?" Chris exclaimed.

Max was unfashionably sporting an outdated stereo on his left shoulder, his right hand casually dipped into his pocket, and his usual short jeans and white socks were now matched with an 80s style light pink Miami Vice jacket with the sleeves rolled up appropriately.

"Please tell me you're not bringing that thing to Worcester, Max. Oh, and Tubbs just called to say he wants his jacket back," joked Chris.

"Why not? It's cool, my brothers," he replied as he pulled a pair of black, plastic sunglasses from his pocket and put them on.

"Jesus, when did you turn into a black man? What's with all this *my brothers* talk?" Chris laughed.

"Please, somebody tell him he can't go to Worcester dressed like that and make sure you also tell him he's got to ditch the stereo!" Stu cried.

"Why can't I go like this? I'm not asking you to hold it, am I?" Max said, not understanding what the problem was.

"No, you're right, but I'm not walking with you looking like that!" Stu snapped back.

"If breakdancers can do it, why can't I?"

"Oh, that's okay then, mate. I forgot that you could breakdance. Where's your mat, then?" Stu said with obvious sarcasm.

"What do I need a mat for? I never said I could breakdance, did I?"

"No, that's right, Esther, you can't. And, by the way, this isn't 1984 either, you prat!"

Stu was getting angrier by the second, but everyone else started to see the funny side of Max's unintentionally comic fashion statement – even the other people who were waiting patiently for the bus started to chuckle to themselves.

"It's okay, Stu, he'll be fine. He can walk behind us," James said just as the bus pulled up to the kerb.

"Don't you dare turn that thing on while we're on the bus!" Stu threatened.

The ride into the city went quietly with Max sitting still, with every attempt to turn on his stereo stopped each and every time by an embarrassed, but vigilant, person in the form of Stu. The second they stepped off the bus and onto the streets of Worcester Max pulled out a pair of headphones from his inside jacket pocket.

"What's he doing now?" questioned Chris.

"I do believe he's about to plug those headphones into his stereo!" answered a completely stunned James.

"Hey, Max!" James said, pulling the headphones away from Max's ears in order to get his attention. "Why didn't you bring your Walkman, mate? I know you've got one; I've seen it."

"The batteries ran out this morning."

"Why didn't you get some more, then?"

"Didn't have time and this was easier."

"Really, *this* was easier?" he said, gesturing wildly at the stereo.

Max nodded and placed the headphones back on and started to move his head to the rhythm of whatever music he was listening to.

"The boy's a nut job, I tell you. A complete and utter basket case. I mean who else goes to bed a normal, white boy and wakes up thinking that they're MC bloody Hammer? The lad's unbelievable, truly, flamin' unbelievable!"

For the next hour and a half the four of them made sure they were at least 20 steps ahead of their increasingly deluded friend. Max seemed happy enough, however, bopping along to his chosen tunes with not a care in the world.

"I'm hungry – who wants a McDonald's?" Chris said, not waiting for an answer and walking straight in.

"Let's sit over there," Stu said as he pointed to a group of seats in the far corner of the restaurant.

"Why there? What's wrong with these here?"

"Have you not seen the girls on the next table?" Stu replied, nodding his head backwards at two very good looking girls and winking with the sureness of a typically confident 16-year-old boy with one thing on his mind.

Stuart made his move with Chris ready and prepared to stroll over a few minutes later. James and Scott's part of the plan would be to get the food and casually sit down with their friends who by now would be well past the 'breaking the ice stage' and on to the 'can I have your number' stage.

As Stu neared his target Max started fiddling awkwardly with his stereo. He pressed the fast forward button and then the rewind button and then listened to the music. He then smiled to himself and turned to Scott and James with his grin now even bigger as he turned up the volume on the stereo fully. He pulled out the headphones jack and sat back in his chair. Nobody expected what happened next as Stu was just about to introduce himself to the bemused girls.

"You're so vain... You probably think this song is about you... You're so vain..." Carly Simon sang, delivered through the blaring stereo that Max was now holding tightly underneath the table.

Stu had a look of death in his eyes with both fists tightly clenched as the words, "I'm going to kill him!" were hissed through equally tightly clenched teeth.

Max didn't hang about and he ran helter-skelter through the busy fast food joint and out onto the street with Stu in hot pursuit. Chris, James, and Scott at first waited behind for a few moments and looked worryingly at each other until they realized that if Stu did catch Max he might actually kill him. They ran as fast as they could out of the establishment and followed the sounds of Max's fading stereo. The song had, however, now changed to the again apt lyrics of Michael Jackson's 'Leave Me Alone'. The further they ran the weirder the situation seemed to become. There they all were, running through the busy streets of Worcester on a Saturday afternoon and chasing the sounds of Michael Jackson – something that none one of them wanted to do, so they stopped. They decided to leave Max to fight for himself. This had been a day full of hilarious events. Well, for Chris, James, and Scott it had been and these were the kind of days that made memories that would last forever.

They finally all met up again an hour or so later in time to catch the last bus home. Max was heard the whole way back continuously professing his innocence: he hadn't meant to pull the headphones out of the now missing stereo; it was all a big mistake. James, Chris, and Scott, however, knew different.

Chapter 7

1994

"Joe, pass me a pair of Axle, size 3F."

"Sure thing, mate," Joe replied.

James had managed to find himself a job in Jones's Boot Maker; a job that he loved. The people were good to work with and he met some interesting characters. The customers would often surprise him with their odd requests.

"Are these sandals waterproof?"

"No, sir, they're sandals."

"Well, have you got any waterproof sandals?"

"No, sir, unfortunately not. We don't sell waterproof sandals. Try Russell & Bromley, I think they sell them."

These were the type of requests that he would face daily, the questions that were impossible to answer.

Every nutty customer they got was sent up to Russell & Bromley – a snobby shop and Jones's competition.

"Do you sell shoes singly? My father only has one leg."

"No, sir, we only sell pairs here. Try Russell & Bromley."

"Do these shoes come in black?"

"They *are* black, sir."

"But I want a different kind of black."

"I'm afraid not, sir. Try Russell & Bromley."

"Do you sell odd shoes here? My one foot is size ten and the other is size nine."

"*Get out!*" James wanted to say but, of course, he could not and had to hold his tongue.

He always looked forward to getting up in the morning, putting on his black shirt and tie, and heading off to work. He liked the independence that it was able to give him. He also liked the fun that he and his workmates would get up to: games that were nothing short of genius resulting from hours of boredom. Frank's speciality was to be blindfolded. He could then tell the make, style, and size of any men's shoe just by the feel of it, just by rubbing his fingers over the punched toe caps or the storm welts. James never saw him get one wrong.

James's idea was named 'Dark Finder'. Yes, each game had to be named as well. The idea behind this particular game was to find a pair of boxed shoes in the dark. The chosen person had to walk down the cold, dank stairway and into the cellar; the lighting was non-existent down there. Each player had to feel their way around the pitch black room, their hands serving as their only guide. This game was really quite scary and not for the fainthearted.

"Joe, you go first," ordered James.

Joe was a cool lad. He had large, round glasses that overlapped his long, slim face and he had a fascination with the number 27 – so much so that he had the number tattooed on his right calf. His belief was that throughout history the number would always pop up. He would often list the names of people who had died at the age of 27 – Jim Morrison, Jimi Hendrix, and the elephant man, John Merrick. He also believed that 27 was a sign for the devil. His explanation was that three times nine equals twenty-seven and nines are just an upside down six and everybody knew that three sixes were a direct line to the beast himself: the number twenty-seven was like Lucifer looking in the mirror. His theory did not quite add up in James's head but he himself knew that not all things could be explained. Maybe Joe did have a point; maybe the number did have a significant part to play in life.

Joe carefully took one step at a time, every movement bringing him that little bit nearer to the darkness. He was in search of a Caterpillar boot: size nine and honey coloured. As he poked and prodded his way underneath the shop floor, he waited for his eyes to acclimatize to the darkness.

James and Carl had another idea in mind. Right at the entrance of the long alleyway that followed on to the basement there was a little hole in the skirting board. It was just about big enough to fit a thin rod through it. At the time James was the only one who knew about it. If he got down on his knees and looked into the gap as if he was peering through a telescope, it was possible to see the deep corners of the stockroom. Not only could he see but he could hear everything – a sense that he needed now that all the lights were off.

James pushed the rod quietly into the hole and waited. He then heard the sound of scuffling making its way across the stone floor beneath him. He pushed the rod deeper into the abyss and the end nudged a heavily stacked pile of shoeboxes. He gave it a slightly harder jab and this time there was the sound of cardboard and leather crashing down directly in front of poor Joe. James and Carl then heard the cries of horror and alarm.

"What the...? Oh my God! Turn the lights on, there's something down here!" Joe shrieked, but his bellows were ignored. "Pl-please, turn the lights on!" he begged, his voice beginning to quiver.

James was still wrapped up in his own hilarity, giving Carl a pat on the back for a prank well done.

"Is he crying, Carl? Damn, I think he's crying!"

James started to feel guilty. Joe had made his own way back upstairs, his palpations almost visible through his shirt and breathing heavily.

"You bastards! Here's your damned boot!"

Joe had still managed to complete his mission through the terror, sliding the box across the imitation leather settees.

"Job well done, Joe!" Carl acknowledged.

"James, can you ring the Edinburgh branch. They have a pair of Camel boots that I want. Get them to put them on the lorry, will you?"

The instruction was hollered from the manager's office, putting an end to their fun.

"Okay, boss. I'll do it right now."

This was another duty that everyone at Jones had to fulfill: the calling up to other branches, with Edinburgh being everyone's least favourite because it was hard to understand their clipped accents. The trilling of the Rs only encouraged the response, *I beg your pardon?* James opened the company phone book and started to dial the number.

"James, can you ge... Sorry, I didn't realize you were on the phone," Carl said and he bustled on by.

"Hello, it's Worcester here. Can you put a pair of Camel Dublin, brown, size 9 on the van, please?"

"No, I can't," replied the voice of a woman.

"I beg your pardon?" James replied, somewhat taken aback by this unexpected response.

He wasn't sure if he had heard her correctly. She didn't sound Scottish, but he could have been wrong.

"I don't have any," she informed him.

"The computer says you do."

"Well, I don't. The computer's wrong," she said with a giggle.

"Who is this?" James enquired.

"Who is this?" she countered.

"It's James, from Worcester."

"Hi, James! I'm Jenny, from Droitwich, currently staying in Edinburgh."

James had dialled the wrong number. He must have pressed the wrong button when Carl briefly interrupted him. Jenny was standing in St Andrew's Square in Edinburgh. She had taken the call of a random ringing phone box, something she had never done before, but felt she had to when the phone started to ring the second she breezed past it; a move that surprised her as much as it did James. The conversation carried on. James found himself talking to her easily. They had so many things in common. Jenny was due to go home in a couple of months and Droitwich wasn't exactly a million miles away. In fact, it was one short train ride from his to hers. After hanging up the phone and making sure he had made plans to meet up with Jenny, James began to slip into one of his elongated thoughts: the notion that if he had not dialled the wrong number he would never have spoken to Jenny, and she would have never spoken to him.

He couldn't believe his luck. She sounded gorgeous. As usual, his thinking went spiralling out of control. What if she wasn't gorgeous? What if she was really ugly? Maybe she was a large girl and she only picked up the phone because nobody liked her and this was her opportunity to chat with someone. James walked back to the phone and pressed redial. He then remembered that it had been a payphone and Jenny would not still be hanging about there. He had no chance of cancelling the date that he had just arranged.

As he replaced the handset, he contemplated not turning up. She might not turn up; she might be thinking the same thing as he was. If she was thinking along the same lines as he was then she might be okay; she might be quite good looking. She might not have three chins and a bottom to match. A chubby person would be happy to get what they could and wouldn't even consider not turning up.

She's going to be lovely!

James felt guilt grow inside him. He should not be thinking this way. Jenny sounded nice enough and that was all that mattered. Whatever she looked like, it did not matter. He would turn up and be pleasant. What were the chances of this sort of thing happening? A wrong number answered by a girl in Scotland who actually lives not 15 miles away: this had to mean something.

The two months flew by. James dressed himself excitably in preparation for his imminent meeting with Jenny. He slapped his dad's aftershave on his face – the aftershave that had been hiding away, forgotten, for as long as he could remember in the unused bathroom cupboard. Tilting his head from side to side in the mirror, he inspected his chin and cheeks for any sign of unwanted facial hair. He worked hard on his hair, making sure the parting was in the exact right place on the left, his black fringe slightly flicked up at the front, and held together with a deluge of hairspray – courtesy of his mum. He then sprayed his Lynx under his arms and all over his green, denim shirt creating a musky smell complemented with Brute. His light blue baggy jeans covered most of his Converse canvas pumps, the fashionable rips and frays showing off his hairy legs. James checked his hair one last time, picked up his mother's vanity mirror and checked his hair at the back.

He saw the baldness that had been left behind after weeks of radiotherapy and the scar poking its way out at the bottom. He sighed and put down the mirror.

"See you later, Mum! I won't be late!" he shouted through the house as he pulled shut the front door.

Sitting alone in the comfy seats in the pub, James looked down at his watch. The time was 7.30 p.m., the evening still light outside and the weather still warm. Ten minutes passed and Jenny was ten minutes late. Every time the saloon-style doors swung open he looked up. He wasn't sure if he actually wanted her to show. He was nervous; this was a girl he had never met. Each overdue minute that passed gave him an opportunity to delve into his unproductive, creative imagination.

"Hi, are you James?"

James had been in a world of his own so he wasn't aware that Jenny had already made her entrance. He had been caught off guard.

"Erm..."

He panicked. Nothing entered his mind; everything he had practised had gone. This was unusual for him. He had always got something rattling around in his brain, but not now.

"Okay, my mistake. Sorry," Jenny said as she turned away.

"Sorry, yes, I'm James."

His words returned just at the last second. She was beautiful. Her long, blonde hair enhanced the red lipstick that lay perfectly on her alluring lips, and her eyes were the brightest blue that he had ever seen. She had the cheeks of a model, and the scent of Giorgio made his heart race.

"You're beautiful."

The words came out before he had a chance to think them through.

"Thank you, James. You're not so bad yourself!" she replied with a grin.

They sat and chatted all evening. Each topic created a new reason for them not to go home. James did not want to go anywhere. He was sure he had already fallen in love; an emotion that he had never felt before. As the night wore on, it was sadly time to leave. James had only minutes to catch the last train home. They both made their way to the exit just as the jukebox started to play *I Swear*: a moment that he would remember for the rest of his life, a time that played out seamlessly. He tenderly leaned forward and asked Jenny if he could kiss her. She nodded with a smile. Her hands naturally moved up and rested on his shoulders as they began to kiss, the song still playing in the background.

"Can I see you again?" James whispered in her ear dreamily.

"Definitely," Jenny answered with certainty and a sigh.

Chapter 8

"I'm pregnant," Jenny blurted out.

"You're *what?*" James asked in a stunned whisper.

"James, I'm pregnant. I've done three tests and I'm definitely pregnant."

Her impatience began to show in her voice.

"Okay," he said quietly, trying to please the other cinemagoers who were getting disgruntled and hissing '*hush*' and '*be quiet*'.

This probably was not the best timing to break such news to him, but, then again, when *would* be the best timing, James thought wryly to himself. As Tom Hanks began one of the most famous lines in film history, Jenny decided to leave the packed out theatre. James quickly followed, apologizing to the people who Jenny had knocked against or tripped over on her way out. Somehow, this was James's fault. He did not quite know how, but it was just his fault according to Jenny.

"What are we going to do, James?" she said as her hands began to tremble.

James's first reply did not go down too well: in his best Forrest Gump drawl he quoted the immortal words, "Oh, Jinny, life is like a…"

Jenny was *not* impressed. He was only trying to lighten the mood, but he quickly moved on to his next best answer.

"I will think of something. I have a job. Maybe we can get a place of our own."

At no time did James think of anything else: this baby was his, a person that he had helped to create. Life is a precious gift, a miracle; something that he knew a lot about. He stayed calm. To him, this was not a problem. He had already done his growing up when he was 14. Having a baby was something to be celebrated, not something to be worried about. Yes, he was only 18 and Jenny was 19 but he knew that he was mature enough to cope with this. He was strong enough for the both of them – all three of them, in fact. Telling his parents, though, was a prospect he did not relish.

"Jenny, I promise you that everything is going to be fine. I will sort it. Please don't worry. I love you."

His words took away the panic and worry that were slowly becoming the only feelings that Jenny had. His guarantees soothed her in a way that nobody else's could. She trusted James completely and she loved him, too.

A week passed and James had decided to tell his parents. First he would approach his dad. His idea being that if he caught him in a good mood (which was most of the time) he could then back up James when he broke the news to his mum. Or, better still, his dad could tell his mum – the best option, in James's view. He would leave Jenny to tell her parents whom he had not met yet. James jumped off the train with a hint of uneasiness. As he walked across the platform, he started to rehearse his speech:

"Dad, the thing is..."

"Dad, stay calm..."

He did not notice the arriving passengers staring at him, each one widening the gap as they neared him. He looked up and saw the strange glares he was getting; a signal for him to shut up and keep walking. He had to pass the new pub on his way home. It was his dad's local and a perfect place to break the news. He looked around inside the pub through the window in the hope of finding his dad sitting in there. *Bingo!* There he was, sitting in a corner between the cigarette machine and the bar. It was his last early shift today. He was bound to be in a good mood. There was no better time to tell him, James thought. Maybe he had already had a couple of pints and his mood would be even better. James took a deep breath and pushed open the bar door with as much self-confidence that he could muster and fixed a big grin on his face.

"You pillock!" was not the reaction James had been expecting or hoping for.

"What are you going to do, James? Looking after a baby is hard. It costs money; money you don't have."

"I have a job, Dad. It's enough to get by and Jenny works as well."

"It's not enough..." His dad paused and started again, "James, what's done is done. There's no going back. Just look after that girl and the baby. Your mum and I will be there for you."

"Thanks, Dad."

That was all he needed – a few words of encouragement from his old man.

"Will you tell Mum for me, please?"

"Oh no, you're not passing that one on to me! You can tell her. Don't worry, I will tell her afterwards that I already know."

"Okay, Dad. Thanks."

James felt nothing, but relief. This was not as hard as he had thought it would be.

"*One down, one to go!*" he thought to himself.

That evening his dad was keeping out of the way. He sat in his office pretending to read a book with his oversized headphones on and the glass-panelled door shut tight. James walked up and tapped lightly on the glass. His dad turned nervously in his chair; he knew what was coming.

James gave the nod. The nod that indicated that this was now the time. The time to man up and face the music. His dad crept up from his chair and tiptoed over to the door.

Pulling it open only slightly, he poked his head through and in a hushed voice said, "I'm here for you."

James felt a little bit calmer now. He walked through the hallway in a manner that screamed out his imminent confession. His mum was sitting at the dining room table with not a care in the world. Her family was all in for the night. She was enjoying the peace and quiet – an atmosphere that was about to change.

"Mum, have you got a minute?" James asked.

"Yes, what's up?"

"Well, the thing is…"

He tussled with his words. He didn't know how to explain.

"What's the matter, James? It can't be that bad, can it?"

"I've got my girlfriend pregnant."

There, he had said it. The words shot from his mouth in an eruption of vocal lava, alleviation now a common feeling in his life. All he needed now was his reinforcement. For a moment his mum said nothing. Her unspoken response simmered, and then it boiled over.

"*Have you heard this?*" she screamed, making her way to her husband's office. "Your son is going to be a father! Did you know?"

Her shouts made the walls shake and the light bulbs seemed to vibrate with fear. James's dad burst out of his office, his face showing a puzzled expression.

"What's going on? Who's having a baby?"

His dad denied all knowledge. He glared at James – a threat, a warning, not to say a word. The tables had turned. James was now backing up his dad: there was no way that his wife would ever find out that he had known a whole day before her.

"How did this happen?" He realized what he had just said, he knew how it had happened, and quickly went on, "I mean... *when* did this happen?"

James was gobsmacked; his dad's denial coming straight from left field, something he had not reckoned on.

His dad mimed the words, "I'm sorry," more than once, his remorse clearly apparent.

James sat and listened to his mum for hours. Once her yelling had stopped she began to talk from the heart. She gave him some good advice. Her final words of the night came with love. As he sat down on the second to last step, his mum sat down beside him. She put her arms around him and cosied in tight.

"Now's the time to be proud, James. There is no greater gift in life than a child of your own. Just be proud."

James started to cry; his mother's words hit him hard. He did not know what the future held for him or Jenny and uncertainty crept in as it had when he was 14. He knew that his situation was self-inflicted, not like before. And this time he had something to look forward to. He started to think about his time in hospital. Not a day went past that he was not reminded of his brain tumour. The shaking was always a reminder. The tiredness also became a factor when his words would mash into one big sound of nothing. He came to the conclusion that because he had gone through the more serious side of life at a young age it had prepared him for this moment. Maybe that was why he got poorly. He believed that everybody had a path, so perhaps this was his.

Why, though, did it have to happen when he was only 18? Was there something else lurking around the corner on his journey? He had already been given the idea that someone was watching over him; guiding him, in fact. He also had the awareness that they knew what would happen 10 or 20 years down the line. There was something he had to do. He was on this Earth to serve a purpose; he just did not know for sure what that purpose was.

Meeting your girlfriend's parents for the first time is always hard. The bogus politeness and the exaggerated please and thank yous were something that most teenagers would have to go through at some point. James would have to meet his girlfriend's parents with the added heaviness of knowing that he had got their daughter pregnant. The strain caused his usual shaking to become much worse than usual.

As he walked up the garden path with Jenny he tried desperately to think of something that would help him get through the next 20 minutes. He did not have time to think as the front door opened suddenly. Jenny's mother just stood there. Her freshly dyed black hair was the first thing that James noticed... and then the face. It did not look happy. No smile to greet the soon-to-be father of her grandchild. James could see only disappointment staring back at him.

"Your father's in the living room, Jenny," she said in a stern manner.

No recognition was given to James whatsoever so he felt the need to introduce himself.

"Hi, I'm James," he said, trying to act and sound confident.

But he failed, and he could hear his voice showing signs of anxiety.

"I know who you are. Jenny's dad is waiting for you in the lounge," she growled.

He took hold of Jenny's hand in the hope that she was coming with him, but instead her mother pulled her into the kitchen. James was left to face the stranger alone. As he fearfully walked up to the living room, he could see that the door was closed; another obstacle that he would have to deal with. It did, however, give him time to compose himself. As he opened the door with trepidation he smelled the strong odour of tobacco. He opened the door a little bit more and entered the smoke-filled room. He began to cough and he waved his hands in front of his face trying not to inhale it. In the corner he could see the outline of a man: a silhouette holding a burning cigarette. This could have been a scene straight from the movies. The man sitting in the chair was the kingpin and James was the lackey about to receive his punishment. James warily checked out the room for any weapons, anything that could be used against him, and then the man spoke, making James jump. He spoke with a deep, threatening, Irish accent.

"So, James, what are your plans?" he questioned, and then took a long drag on his cigarette.

"I don't know, sir. I have a job and I love your daughter," James replied, his feet firmly rooted to the spot.

Jenny's dad never moved from the chair, he just bombarded James with questions and accusations. He just listened until her dad said something that he did not agree with.

"Do you know what I think, James? I think that you will stay around for six months, maybe even a year, and then you will bugger off. You will bugger off, leaving my daughter to raise that child on her own."

James spoke for the second time, his tone now assertive.

"No! No, I won't. You don't know me. I love your daughter more than anything. There is no way that I would ever leave her to bring up my child on her own."

Jenny's dad leaned forward menacingly, his face becoming visible through the smoke with a shaft of light shining through the curtain and onto his cheek.

"Okay, James, you prove me wrong then."

His voice lightened and then he leisurely reclined back into the chair, turning his glance away from James. James started to speak, but then realized quickly that the meeting was now over. He turned around and walked away. He felt proud of himself. Yes, he had been scared and intimidated at first, but he never let those feelings

144

win. He meant everything he had said to Jenny's father. He and Jenny were in this together.

Callum was born on the 1st of August 1995. He was two weeks late and it was a breech delivery but he was healthy. When James looked into his son's bright, blue eyes for the first time he melted. His love grew stronger in an instant. There was nothing he would not do to protect this baby. He was now living for someone else. He now had a family and his job was to look after them. It was a duty that he was proud to do, just the way his mother had explained it to him.

Over the next two years the family grew from three to four with the addition of Ben. Ben arrived on time, on the 20th of March 1997. James felt the same way as he did when Callum had been born. He was an innocent child needing love – love that he would certainly receive from both his young parents.

***

James and Jenny did not really get the chance to go out much. In fact, it was so rare that when they were asked to attend James's boss's leaving party (it turned out to be a pub crawl) they did not hesitate to get a babysitter. It's amazing how something so small can get two people so excited but that is exactly what they were – excited.

"Jenny, that's the fifth outfit you've tried on!"

James was exasperated for the umpteenth time. He was losing count and beginning to lose his patience.

"I know, but I want to look good!" Jenny replied, still checking herself up and down in the tall mirror that leant against the wall just to the left of her ever-so-bored husband.

"You do look good, Jenny. No, you look fantastic… You *always* look fantastic."

James thought he had better change his reply to 'fantastic' if only to avoid the questioning that his wife would undoubtedly grill him with for saying *just* good.

"Thank you," Jenny replied with a knowing smile, "but I think I prefer the black top and jeans with the boots. What do you think?"

"Isn't that what you tried on fir–? Yeah, I liked that look. Let's go with that, then," he sighed in resignation.

James was desperately trying not to complicate his answers or in any way get into trouble with his responses. Jenny took a further half an hour to get ready. James just had to wait patiently.

The occasional sigh he emitted was only followed with the reply, "Don't rush me, James!"

This was definitely something he had no chance of doing. No man should ever attempt to hurry his wife or partner in such a strategic operation as trying on clothes!

As the doorbell rang, James was already halfway down the stairs. He had heard his parent's car pull up outside. After almost tripping over one of his children's toys that lay dangerously on the bottom step he turned back and bent down to remove it out of harm's way. He opened the front door quietly, immediately putting his finger over his pursed lips. No more was needed to be said: the children were fast asleep. Well, at least for the next few hours anyway; they would often wake up inappropriately at any given time. This was something that no matter how hard that Jenny and James tried they just could not get used to. It was going to be nice to get a bit of peace and quiet away from their children just for once, no matter how much they loved and adored them.

James led his mum and dad into the living room and quietly explained where everything was and relayed the strange sleeping pattern that his children had decided to adopt. He began to tell the story that only a few days ago he had been walking the streets at two in the morning in a desperate attempt to get Ben to fall sleep.

Turning his head at the sound of Jenny walking down the stairs, James went back into the hallway and thought how beautiful his wife looked. He gave her a more than approving smile as she slowly took each step perfectly one at a time. James often had this feeling about Jenny; there were times when she just took his breath away with her beauty. Tonight, however, she looked simply amazing. Her blonde hair seemed to bounce softly and in slow motion as she made her way to be at James's side. They were now ready to go and with hushed goodbyes off they went to enjoy the evening.

It was dark and slightly damp. The air had a cold snap to it as the couple made the short walk into the city centre. Arriving later than everyone else at the Slug and Lettuce pub, James could not resist reminding Jenny why they were late and next time it might be an idea if she started to get ready about three hours earlier than she had tonight. James put his hand in his pocket in order to buy their first drinks of the night.

"James, let's buy our own drinks tonight; we can't afford to get in rounds," Jenny whispered.

"Yeah, okay. I had already thought of that. We can't go mad either, okay?" James replied just as quietly.

Just as James started to order the drinks a deep voice bellowed from behind him, "The first drinks are on me, James. You can get the next ones."

It was George, James's boss. He knew exactly how much James earned but obviously didn't have that much sympathy for his bank balance situation. He was quite often the person who would brag about his own income although he was not a stingy man and would quite often be known to put his hand in his own pocket. James thought that perhaps he was just wrapped up in his own night and the fact that James and Jenny did not have much money simply slipped his mind.

"Erm, okay," James answered as he gave his wife a questioning glance.

Jenny could only shrug her shoulders and smile disapprovingly because she knew that James had been put on the spot. Their secret communication came very naturally and words were not always needed. It had been talked about only a few hours previously at work that this night was only going to be a few quiet drinks and then possibly back to George's house for a bite to eat and a surprise that would turn out to be little bit more than just a surprise.

Most of the staff had turned up. Joe was sitting quietly in the corner chatting and chortling with Carl, but James did not recognize the girl who was with him. James remembered that only a few days before a different girl had met him from work, giving him a big kiss outside the shop before they made their way to wherever Carl had decided to take her. All his girls were very attractive but not always the brightest tools in the box, but Carl was not a conversationalist anyway.

"All right, James. All right, Jenny. This is Tabatha," Carl announced proudly.

"The last one was called Tracy, if you're wondering, James," Joe blurted out before James could say hello. Joe continued, "And the one before that was call–"

"Okay, Joe, give it a rest," Carl quietly ordered with an air of aggression and an elbow to Joe's ribs as he moved back and pushed himself awkwardly into his seat.

Joe was certainly quiet now, but Tabatha was starting to look a little perturbed by the mention of Carl's possible long string of girlfriends.

"Who's Tracy?" she questioned.

James could see that Carl had yet again got himself into hot water so, rather than sit by and watch, he and Jenny took the opportunity to move themselves away from the forthcoming argument, indicating to Joe that it was probably a good idea if he did the same before he got another dig in his ribs, or worse. All three of them started up their own conversation on a separate table and the battle commenced in the background with occasional turns of the head from Joe to see who was winning. Amazingly, it wasn't long before Tabatha and Carl were kissing passionately but, just as amazingly, it wasn't long before Tabatha stood up and slapped Carl hard across the face before walking out of the pub.

Clearly embarrassed, Carl stood up and moved over to the empty seat next to James.

"What happened, mate?" Joe quizzed with an obvious smirk across his childish face.

"Well, I had it sorted and explained that Tracy was an old girlfriend and all was fine. That's when she started kissing me."

Carl really didn't want to explain the rest but after a lot of badgering from Joe, James, and Jenny he could not evade the questioning and told them the rest.

"After we kissed I told her that I really like her and that she was the only girl for me. She said I was the only man for her and all was hunky dory."

"Then what?" Jenny asked with her impatience at Carl's inability to get to the point beginning to show.

"Then I called her *Tamara*," Carl said sheepishly.

With a laugh on the brink of erupting James blurted out, "Who the hell is Tamara?"

"She was the one after Sandra but the one before Tulisa... You know, Joe, the redhead."

Carl gestured with his hands at the same time in front of his chest to indicate that she also had rather large breasts; something he was sure Joe would remember. Joe just looked puzzled as he looked over at James and Jenny and shook his head and rolled his eyes.

"Hang on, Carl. Are you going through that alphabet thing with your girlfriends again?" James asked half-jokingly.

"Yeah, I am, mate. I managed to get to T without any problems. I really liked her as well," Carl said feeling somewhat sorry for himself.

James, Jenny, and Joe could do nothing but burst out laughing and Carl's next comment made them laugh even more: "I had a Z worked out but I was struggling a bit with an X."

Carl was totally serious which made his self-inflicted comic situation even funnier. Most of the night after that point was just one laugh after another with Carl providing just the right amount of self-teasing in each and every pub that they all visited. The conversation later took on a more serious tone, though. Again, it started with Carl's alphabet dating and quickly moved on to fate. This was something that James had some understanding of on some level.

"Why can't you just wait for the right person, Carl?" Joe asked, his voice slightly slurred with alcohol and his head wobbling gently. "Don't you believe in fate?" he continued.

"Fate? Don't make me laugh – there's no such thing!"

Carl seemed so sure in his disbelief, but James felt compelled to respond.

"How do you know it doesn't exist?"

James took Carl's answer personally and it showed in his tone.

"Calm down, James, we all know how you met Jenny! That's what people call a coincidence or luck, mate. It certainly wasn't fate, though," Carl retorted with the same attitude as James.

James wanted to argue with Carl but he decided not to bother. He wanted to tell him about his time in hospital, the voice he had heard, and the way the tumour was eventually found by accident, but he realized that it was not the time or the place. Although he had the confidence of a few drinks behind him he still managed to stop himself.

He was not sure why, but he did say one thing: "Nobody knows what's around the corner. Fate is real. Think about the things that have happened in your life."

"What things, James? Come on, tell me. I make my own destiny, not someone else. Not God or whoever else you believe is up there pulling the strings. God does not exist and neither does fate."

Before James could answer Carl, Jenny found herself intervening with, "I think everyone has had a little too much to drink tonight. How about we change the subject?"

Carl ignored her suggestion and added another of his blinkered views: "What do you think, James? Do you think that people's paths collide for a reason? Do you think that collision was planned and that in some way they are going to change the world? Ha! Ha! Ha!"

Carl's view had quickly turned to ridicule.

"Not change the world, no, but rather be a part of it; an event that might lead onto the next," James calmly replied. He had started to realize that it did not matter what Carl thought or believed. He knew different and that's all he cared about. "Okay, let's go, shall we?" James then said.

"No, you started this so let's finish the conversation."

Carl took another swig from his almost empty pint of lager, getting drunker by the minute.

"All right, Carl, calm it down. James has his opinion and you have yours. Let's leave it there, eh?"

Joe had also had enough of Carl's attitude by now. Carl snarled and confidently sat back in his chair. He was sure that he had won the argument with his words being the last. To James, though, it no longer mattered. He knew what had happened all those years ago and the events before and after. The whole heated discussion just got him thinking about what *was* in his future; it was something he thought about often. He was sure that it was going to be good but there was always that niggling feeling that maybe it would not be. The confidence that had been brutally taken away from him all of those years ago still had not fully returned and it probably never would.

The party, or pub crawl as it had turned out to be, was starting to come to an end and everyone who was still standing began talking about going back to George's house. By this point everyone was hungry. They needed something to soak up the lager, wine, or whatever choice of alcohol they had chosen that night.

"One more drink here and then we are all going back to my house," George ordered.

He was met with a chorus of both approving and disapproving shouts from the gang. James, who had not had a drink for a while, made his way to the bar and noticed Joe looking ever-so-slightly confused at his drunken reflection in the mirror that stretched right across the wall behind the bar.

"You okay there, Joe?" he asked.

"Yesh, but who's that on the other side of the bar in the other room?"

His excessive intake of cider was now affecting his common sense and speech.

"Who are you talking about? What room? There's no one on the other side of the bar," James answered with a giggle.

"*Him*, James, *him!* He looks just like *me!* Shh!"

Joe's initial shouting turned to a whisper and then back to a shout. James could not resist going along with Joe's imaginary doppelgänger.

"Oh yeah, I see him, too. He's even wearing the same clothes as you, mate."

"Hey, James, heesh even wearing the shame clothes as me, too!"

This was followed by a little hiccup and then a loud burp as Joe looked at and inspected the white shirts and black jackets that he and the other man had both chosen to wear that very same evening. Joe tugged and pulled at his collar but as he did so this only convinced him that the imposter was now somehow taking the micky out of him by copying his every move. James turned back and called Jenny over to the bar with a small sign with his hand.

"Hey, Jenny, there's a bloke on the other side of the bar who looks exactly like Joe and he's wearing the same clothes as well. Do you know him at all?"

Jenny quickly realized what was going on and shot back, "Can't say that I do, but he looks just like you, Joe. Wow, that's amazing!"

In his inebriated state Joe failed to notice that there was also a man who looked just like James and a woman who looked just like Jenny on the other side of the bar, as well. For the time being it really wasn't worth confusing Joe anymore, although it really was very tempting to do so.

"Oi, barman! Sorry... Shh! Sorry, barman! Who's that man in the other room?" Joe asked, pointing from the barman then to the mirror and then back to the barman.

"What room?" the barman asked in a way that showed that he had been asked the question many times before.

The barman seemed to slide along the bar to Joe in a blur and then he leaned over and explained to James and Jenny that it was much funnier if you take away the idea of another room.

"*That room, there!*" Joe cried and then made his way slowly and clumsily out of the pub only to come straight back in and up to the bar again.

As soon as he did this he again stumbled back outside. On his second return to the bar he started to shout out at the bar itself in bewilderment.

"Where hash the room gone? It's not outside. He's still there! Who ish he, James? I'm scared now. James! Jenny! Carl!"

Joe turned around in a panic and yelled, "Where's Carl gone?"

By this point the entire pub was in hysterics. Joe looked again at the mirror, or the 'vanishing room' as he now knew it.

"Carl, I shee you!"

Carl had also had far too much to drink and was by now propping up the bar at the other end of the pub, but Joe could only see him in the mirror. In reality, Carl was being obscured by a huddle of large men in everyone else's normal world.

"James, can we go now? Can you find Carl?" Joe bleated.

"Yes, Joe, let's go. Will you be okay going to George's house?"

"Pleash, let's just go!" Joe wailed.

Arriving at George's house, James and Jenny took it upon themselves to look after Joe. They delicately and wearily helped him step down from the taxi and then over to the house.

"I need the loo!" Joe exclaimed.

"We'll be in the house soon. Can you wait for a second?" James said as he turned around to see Joe disappearing alone into the night.

"Joe, where are you going?" Jenny asked.

"To use the bathroom," Joe hiccupped back.

"That's not the bathroom, that's the garden," she replied.

"I'll wait here for him, Jenny. You go inside," James suggested.

Joe continued to walk away. Well, it was more of a crawl at points but it got him to where he needed to be. With his trousers now wrapped around his knees, Joe crouched down and then lowered his bottom to the ground. James could just about make out what Joe was about to do and started to walk towards him.

"Joe! *Joe!* You can't do that there! No, please! Oh, God, no!"

"I'm not doing what you think I'm doing. I always go to the loo sitting down," Joe explained as if it were normal and almost fell over as he turned his to head to face James.

"What, even outside? Seriously, mate, it's just weird!"

"What's that noise?" Joe suddenly yelped.

"What noise?" James asked. "Are you hearing things now? Come on, let's get inside. It's freezing out here."

Joe stood up as slowly and as quietly as he could which, to be honest, was not as quiet as it could have been. His body never made a sound as he pulled his boxer shorts back up. It was his mouth that James was convinced got him into trouble. With only his pants pulled up and his trousers still around his knees, Joe began to run as fast as he could. Well, as fast as a man being impaired by an unfortunate trouser situation could run. To be fair he was doing extremely well, all things considered. James could not yet see what Joe was running away from, but it was not long before he began to hear something: one thud quickly followed by another and then another.

"Oh, my God!" James muttered to himself. "It's a–"

George's new home had only really just been finished being built with equally large grounds to match. These grounds covered at least one acre for a reason; a reason that George was just about to explain.

"I bought the grounds from my father-in-law. He has the next house along the way and the plan is that I'm going to join him in his own business. He's been breeding–"

"Kangaroos!" Jenny finished for him.

"Yes, how did you know? I haven't mentioned them to anyone yet. That's amazing!" George marvelled.

"There are two kangaroos in your front garden and they're chasing Joe," Jenny said, pulling herself closer to the window with everyone else following suit.

"Oh no, this has happened once before! They've got through the fence again!" George said with more concern for his kangaroos than for poor, old Joe.

"Joe, come this way," James instructed as he showed Joe a possible escape route through a garden gate.

Even though James was extremely worried about Joe he could not get the image out of his mind of a penguin with thick glasses being pursued by a deranged kangaroo. From the window it must have looked even funnier: a silent movie being played on a large television screen with the outside lights providing the slight intermission between each prolonged scene. Joe managed to throw himself headfirst through the gate and behind James who, in a panic, frantically slammed the gate shut behind them both.

"I bet you've sobered up now, Joe," remarked an out-of-breath James with an almost unwanted smile on his face.

"Erm, I think so. Thanks, mate," Joe replied as he wiped the mud and sweat from his face.

Out of nowhere it hit Joe at the strangest time possible: "Was that a mirror in the pub?"

"Ha! Yes, that was a mirror... but I haven't a clue who that man was!"

As they both walked wearily and breathlessly into the house they were met by a huge round of applause with both of them bowing to their audience; their impromptu entertaining display was a hit with their fans. George eventually managed to round up his kangaroos, after a fashion, but nobody seemed to notice how long it took him though.

The slightly longer walk home seemed to pass by very quickly, but not before James and Jenny stopped to admire the stars. This was something they had never really done before together. Yes, it was cold but the sky was so amazingly clear and the stars seemed even closer than usual. Apart from the little argument with Carl, the night had been brilliant throughout and romantic at the end.

It was Jenny who first noticed that their children's bedroom light was on and this could only mean one thing: the children were wide awake. As they both neared the front door they joked about turning around and going back to the pub.

"Hello!" they both called out at the same time, but not too loudly, still hoping that their children may still be asleep.

"Your mother's just this second got Ben back to sleep. He only woke up about an hour ago so you might be lucky," James's dad said with a tired smile.

"Thanks, Dad."

"Did you have a good time?" James's mum asked as she tiptoed down the stairs.

"Brilliant, Mum, thanks. Joe got chased by a kangaroo! I'll explain tomorrow, though, as I'm sure you want to get home," James replied.

"Thanks ever so much for having the boys tonight," Jenny said appreciatively.

James's mother and father grabbed their coats and left, but not before giving Jenny and James a big kiss and cuddle.

"Do you want to go straight to bed?" James asked Jenny with a suggestive wink.

"I would rather catch up on some sleep, to be honest, James."

"I'm glad you said that because I'm absolutely shattered!"

They both laughed and made their way straight up to bed, but as soon as their heads hit their pillows a loud cry came from the boys' bedroom.

***

James and Jenny were still very much in love. Yes, there were days when they argued over the smallest of things and there were days when the fights meant something. Money was the root of a lot of the nasty words that were exchanged; money that they never had, money that they needed.

James worked hard at the shoe shop. He had earned himself a promotion, allowing them to breathe just that little bit easier. It did mean, though, that every so often he would have to go away overnight. This was a part of his job that he did not like. He hated leaving his family. He hated leaving Jenny to cope on her own. It was Catch 22: if he did not go away it meant no extra money; if he did go away it meant an argument when he got back home. Jenny knew that he was doing the best he could but having him going away was hard on her. This is something that most married couples must do, why should they be any different? James was on his way to fast track management and this was a sacrifice he had to make in order to provide a better future for his family.

One of James's nights away would often be in Birmingham, the city where he had spent five of the hardest weeks of his life. Because of the connections he did not really like going there. It brought back a lot of memories. Some he laughed about, but most he didn't.

As he strolled through the city centre, with his briefcase firmly gripped in his right hand, the hustle and bustle was a million miles away from the small town where he now lived. Burger vans were sitting on every corner, the aroma only encouraging people to part with their money whether they were hungry or not.

As he neared his place of work he took the final sip from his takeaway hot chocolate, throwing it away in the bin that was conveniently placed to the side of the shop. James pushed the large, glass doors open with enthusiasm greeting staff and customers alike. As he passed cheerfully through the shop he almost did not notice the chaos of shoe-filled cartons that lay in wait for him – a job that would almost certainly take up his whole day.

"Okay then, let's get to work, shall we?"

The smile did not come easily. After hours and hours of pair-checking each and every box of shoes, James designated two members of staff to find a place in the stockroom. The long, tiring day was finally over, James was tired, and the hour was late. He did not fancy a repetition of the day he had just had but he knew that tomorrow would only bring more of the same.

He walked away from the building with pleasure. He could not wait to fall into his cheap hotel room bed, courtesy of Jones the boot makers. He climbed under the covers with satisfaction and his only thought was sleep. He was shattered but, as much as he tried, he just could not fall asleep. After a few hours, he gave up and decided to leave the hotel for a short while. Maybe he would get something to eat, or perhaps he might just walk.

Chapter 9

1986

Ohio

The crying seemed almost as if it had, in some way, been rehearsed. It only seemed this way because it was something that Sam had been witnessing quite a lot over the past few months, even though her parents had tried to hide their true emotions from her. They tried to protect her in some way from what was always going to be the end result. They knew that, at some point, this anguished day would come. They had tried to prepare themselves for it but, no matter how long you have known something will happen, you can never really can.

As the words were spoken by the doctor, Sam's parents just listened; a last ditch hope and a desperation that this was not going to finish with the line, "I'm so sorry."

There was no hope left. There was no last minute miracle that they had been praying for, praying for every day for a long time.

"I'm so sorry," was said with feeling and they were the words they heard that day that were so final yet so resounding. The sentence that meant they would never again see their darling son in the way that they would always remember him: running, laughing, and enjoying life, without a care in the world. A healthy teenager looking ahead to the rest of his life.

They turned away from the doctor as they tried to take in what he had just told them. Time seemed to stand still. The people around them carried on with what they were doing. A woman carrying flowers to visit a loved one; a man holding two cups of coffee made his way around Sam and her parents, almost annoyed that they were blocking his path. The hospital was busy and the sounds of people laughing, squeaking wheelchairs, and the bleeping and chiming of hospital equipment could be heard by everyone except Sam's parents.

Everything went quiet. Objects moved silently, people's lips chattered in conversation but no sound was heard. The shock-induced deafness only ceased when they looked down and saw their daughter. Sam looked up at her parents for answers. Even though she was only seven years old she was dreading what those answers might be.

She knew that her older brother had been in hospital for a long time and that every day she had watched him slowly change. He became quieter, weaker, and his appearance was something that she would never forget. His body had got thinner and his once thick, black hair had simply disappeared. Through the eyes of a child, she knew that things were not right. She was aware that this was not the way things should be. Even seeing him lying there in his hospital bed every day for months on end she never once thought that her beloved brother would be snatched away from her. The brother who had always been there for her; the brother who every time he glanced at his little sister did so with love and gratefulness, a thank you for the day that she was brought into the world.

She adored her brother and he adored her. Sam had been just as important to her brother as he had been to her, but now she was about to be told that he was no longer with her and those days together would never happen again.

"Sam…"

Her mother stumbled across her words. Her voice started to break as she wiped away the flowing tears from her eyes; the tears that she had cried so many times before and the tears she simply could not hold back no matter how hard she tried.

Sam just watched and listened as her hand tightly gripped her father's coat. Her mother ran her hand down her husband's arm and gave him a look; a look asking how she could possibly deliver the explanation that their son, her brother, had passed away.

"Mum, what's happened?" Sam asked.

"It's your brother," she said as she knelt down to her daughter, their eyes connecting the second they were at the same level.

She lovingly placed her shaking hand on the side of Sam's face and moved it up through her long, brown hair. Her lips began to tremble as she dropped her head in anguish. It took a great deal of inner strength but she found it quickly for her daughter's sake. She took a deep breath, steeling herself, and lifted her head back up preparing to continue.

Sam pointed at the glass panel door where her brother lay beyond and said, "What about him, Mum? I can see him; he's sleeping."

Her mother hesitated in answering, collecting her thoughts. She had to be strong, just for a moment, while she delivered the terrible news. She had to find a way of explaining that he was not sleeping.

"Yes, honey, he's sleeping, but it's not a normal kind of sleep. This sleep is going to last for a very long time; he might never wake up."

This seemed like the best way to describe what had happened – a way that could even help them, as parents, to even contemplate coming to terms with what was happening and an easier choice of words that were not too harsh to say that her brother was dead.

Sam knew what her mother meant and she also somehow knew to hold back any questions. She never cried at that time but neither did she say a word. Her silence said it all as she looked deeply into both of her parents' eyes. Their eyes looked the same: empty, and the sparkle and joy that Sam had known all her life had gone only to be replaced by... nothing. Or was it that Sam had never come across this feeling before? None of them had felt like this before. It was an understanding of confusion for everyone – they all knew *what* had happened but explaining *how they felt* was impossible.

The long drive home that afternoon was just as quiet. The reasoning for this day would never be truly understood by anyone. It was then that Sam could no longer keep quiet. Before she spoke she watched her parents and waited for the right moment to say something, but there was no right time – there never would be.

"Why did Gareth die, Mum?"

She changed her position and glanced out the window. She had asked the question but by not looking at her mother she would not see her reaction. Her mother was momentarily startled by her daughter's voice suddenly breaking the deafening silence. Sam had not spoken a word for the last hour, but she was only asking the question that they all wanted an answer for – why did Gareth die?

"Sam, Gareth had been very poorly for quite a long time... but I don't know why he died."

Of course she knew the medical reasons, after the constant reminders and explanations from the doctors, but this was not enough. Why did he actually have to die? No parent should lose a child; it is unnatural. This question, this non-understanding, would be the thing that they would ask themselves for the rest of their lives. They would try to learn to live with it in some kind of abnormal existence, but they would never, ever get over it. Nobody *gets over* losing a loved one, someone that they themselves would give their own life for.

Sam had no more questions for the next few hours. She chose, instead, to remember her brother in her own way. She thought about the times that he would have to babysit her even though all his friends were going out, the games in the park and the ones at home. She remembered him laughing and she remembered him crying, the crying that she sometimes, in her own way, tried to comfort him with.

All it sometimes took was a cuddle; a cuddle to say, "You're my brother and I will love you forever."

She remembered as much as she could. It was an attempt to never forget him even though, of course, there was no way she ever would. She started from when she could first remember, right up until the time that she wanted to forget – the times that she had witnessed when, she now realized, his life had been almost over. An instance came to her thoughts of the last time they had giggled together. This would be the last time that they shared anything together and possibly a big part in her everlasting memory of him.

She remembered something that gave her the chance to lovingly mock her brother, not knowing it would be for the last time. The day before, Sam had arrived at her brother's hospital room just a few minutes before her parents. She had been eager, as usual, to spend time with him, to listen to his stories, to hold his hand, and to cuddle him. As she had walked in she noticed that Gareth was talking to someone. She carried on to the other side of the room without interrupting and looked to see who it could possibly be sitting on the old hospital chair that had been pushed back against the white wall in the corner of the room; the chair that she had made her own, as many people would have done before and many would do after her, but there was nobody there, just the chair.

"Who are you talking to?" She asked, intrigued, the laughter begging to be released from her mischievous lips.

"Nobody," Gareth answered with a smile beginning to develop between the tubes that she had unknowingly become used to ignoring.

"Yes you were. Are you talking to yourself again, Gareth? Remember when I found you talking to the mirror about Helen Cartwright last year?"

Gareth started to laugh quietly. He, too, remembered that day; a day that he would rather have forgotten.

"I was just asking myself some questions, that's all, Saman*ta*."

Sam had now forgotten about her brother talking to himself and was now annoyed that he had called her Saman*ta* – a joke shared between the two of them from a time when Sam was learning to speak but every attempt to say her own name ended with her saying Saman*ta*, and Gareth had never let her forget it.

"It's Saman*tha*, not Saman*ta*!" she retorted cheekily.

"Hey, you said that name first, not me... Saman*ta!*"

"Stop it! It's only because I couldn't speak properly when I was little," she replied as she climbed onto the chair and rested on her knees.

"It's okay, I'm only joking... Saman*ta.*"

He just couldn't resist one last poke.

As the memory started to fade Sam pushed herself back into the car seat, still staring out the window. She desperately tried to remember what it was that she had heard her brother say. She went over and over in her mind the moment she walked through the swing doors. She remembered that she never actually pushed open the doors – they had been held open by a fire extinguisher. It was something she had not taken in at the time, but why had she forgotten what he had said?

At that moment her concentration was interrupted as she watched her mother reach over to the car radio; a possible attempt to break the silence, maybe, or a reason just to do anything to try to take away the numbness that she was feeling, the numbness they were all feeling.

The first words that came from the radio were, "It's a gloomy evening and it's six o'clock. You are listening to—"

"Gosh, is that the time?" Sam's dad remarked.

He did not actually care what the time was and Sam could hear it in his voice – he was just saying something, anything, for the sake of it.

Is this the way the healing process starts? A simple question of normality in a situation of pure tragedy. The song that followed next was not simply ignored or an unwanted melody that seemed to just linger in the air. It was a tune that fitted sadly to the unintentional quietness that was all around – Simon and Garfunkel's 'The Sound of Silence'. It was a song that seemed to make their feelings more noticeable: a touch, a look, or a dip of the head when random lyrics reminded them of random moments gone by.

Sam would never forget those emotions. She would learn to grow into them. Day by day she would understand more about the anger and how the anger turned to despair, eventually going through the whole cycle of emotions. She would watch as her parents time and time again pulled themselves up from the depths of a mental suffering that they would, for many years, find creeping upon them. A reminder of their son – a sound or a smell was all it took – sometimes just a word.

It is weird how a meaningless thing can transform itself in a person's mind to be of great meaning, if they want it to be. This is a feeling that Sam could not fathom but she found herself doing the same things as her mother and father. One thing that she would always do was remember that car journey every time she heard that song again.

Her father's comment was the trigger that reminded Sam what it was that Gareth had said – he had simply asked the question, "Is it time?" Then there had been a small pause as if someone else was in the room and the reason why she had thought that someone was there with him. He had then said the words, "Okay, I'm ready."

It was then that Sam tried, in her own mind, to come to terms with what was happening and to understand what he had been talking about. It was also a time that would make her realize that great things don't always last forever: a harsh reality in the mind of a seven-year-old girl, an event that should never happen to someone so young.

As the song played quietly in the background Sam looked at her parents one at a time trying to take in what they might be thinking and how they were feeling. She herself did not know how to feel. She did not have the capabilities yet to know the correct way to react and she did not even know that there was no right or wrong way how people should deal with this. She watched her parents for some kind of natural guidance, that's all she could think to do, but they themselves were looking to each other for that unspoken support.

On the radio Sam heard the words, "*People talking without speaking, people hearing without listening.*" It was a moment in life explained at a time when it was needed. Sam learned that day that a look between loved ones can say so much more than a million verbalized words could ever do.

The house was quiet as the three of them entered it that night with the car keys being the only sound heard as Sam's dad placed them down in the bowl that sat on the table at the bottom of the stairs, clanging against Gareth's motorbike keys that had not been touched for months. Sam's dad stopped and turned back to the keys on the table. He picked up the motorbike keys and began to cry. The times he had warned his son of the dangers on the road, and how careful he had to be, flashed through his mind. He recalled how many times he had said he did not want to visit his son in hospital, or worse. The tears came in floods as his raw emotions took control. Sam's mother just seemed to stand by and watch for a few seconds and then she started to cry, too. How they wished that they were now sitting on the couch waiting and worrying until their gorgeous boy returned home.

Still they only asked themselves one question: *why?* Sam again found herself asking questions out loud. It was as if she was some sort of a vessel for what her parents were thinking but she had a child's innocence to verbalize them.

"Could we have stopped this, Mum?" she asked.

Perching on the edge of the couch her mother explained that they had tried everything they possibly could. It was almost as if she had asked herself the same question many times and she had the answers off by rote now. But every answer she gave herself created another question and every question created an unneeded amount of doubt. Did they do everything? Did they ask the right questions? Were those questions to the right people? They knew deep down that there was nothing else they could have done but it did not stop them from asking. All they could do now was try to come to terms with what had just happened. They needed to do the right thing for Sam; the daughter they would have to find strength for, the same strength that they would have to find for themselves in a place where that exact courage was hidden. With each other's help they would have to find it.

The question that Sam had just asked – "Could we have stopped this?" – was to have a lasting effect on her life. It was a question that would, in time, help her to discover the person she wanted to be and the question itself would be something that one day she might be able answer on some sort of level.

Sam's thoughts, yet again, turned to the things that her brother had said to himself. Somehow they seemed to fit with the things she was thinking. She would now never forget what he had said that day. She would never forget *the way* the words were spoken but she would struggle, however, to understand what they actually meant for a very long time.

Life was never quite the same after that day. How could it be? It was as if Sam's parents had to start their relationship all over again. For a time they did not speak to one another. Their conversations were conducted by sighs, looks, and lots of crying. If they did happen to talk then the words only seemed to get in the way of what they truly needed to say. But they still loved each other very much and their love for Sam was always there, too. In fact, they seemed to put all of their attention towards her. She was now their main target for affection.

Sam was becoming a distraction for her parents to focus on. It took time to rebuild what they once had together, but they always knew that they would get it back, somehow. There was no way they could blame each other for the untimely death of their son but they were afraid of their own deep and dark feelings, too afraid to speak about them. They each had to find a way to get rid of the anger inside, or at least find a way to live with it, otherwise it would eat them up and destroy them. They knew they owed it to themselves after all they had been through, and they owed it to little Sam.

There was not a day that went past that they did not think about Gareth. At first they could only think of the way he was the last time they saw him: the image of their child just lying there in pain, a pain that they never felt themselves. The only pain they had was from feeling helpless as they could do nothing but look on as he wasted away, hour by hour.

Those thoughts gradually changed. Each time their memories were triggered by something or someone they would think of the good times that Gareth had given them. At first they had to train themselves to do this by pushing out the bad reminders and replacing them with new memories and after time, with practice, the immediate thoughts were happy ones. It was this way of thinking that started to bring back the recollection of normality into their lives. Things would never be the same, but things could be different in a good way. It was the guilt that, for a long time, stopped them from living differently, the guilt that they were still living after their son had died, but until they came to terms with that they were stuck in a living purgatory.

Sam hardly ever spoke of that day. Yes, she often talked about her brother, but not about *that* day. As she grew older she realized that she wanted, in some way, to help others who might be going through this illness. She wanted to know and understand what had happened to her brother and, in doing so, she found a new thirst for knowledge; a knowledge to find the answers to why and how. This desire to learn would lead her to a place one day that could answer some questions and put her mind at rest.

***

"Hi, Jules," said an American woman as she was driving through the quiet streets of a late night in Birmingham. "Is Mum there?" she asked, continuing to speak into her mobile phone.

"Hi, Sam, how are you getting on?" her mother eagerly questioned.

"Yeah, Mum, it's good. I'm under a new doctor now. He's teaching me a lot about—"

Her sentence was cut short. Sam could see a car pull out in front of her. She tried desperately to swerve out of its way but, at the speed she was going, it was too late.

***

James wandered tiredly down the darkened street, wrapping his coat tightly around himself, but the cold air was sneaking in wherever it could. He tried not to think of anything; he just needed sleep. He did not want to go back to the hotel room, thinking things over in the way he normally did.

Suddenly, he found himself instinctively placing his hands behind his head and momentarily losing his footing at the sound of an enormous bang behind him. He turned around and tried to see what it was he needed protection from. Behind him he could see the crumpled result of two cars that had just crashed into one another. He started to walk towards the carnage, his heart began to race, and his adrenaline pumped like never before. His steps gradually got faster and faster until he was sprinting. He could smell the overwhelming stench of petrol as he neared the wreckage.

Without any regard for his own safety, he sprang into action. He ran up to the first car just as a flame began to flicker from the overturned engine. He could see the desperation on the driver's face. The seatbelt was keeping her from hitting the dented roof. She was trying to turn around to the back seat. James followed her eyes, momentarily pausing with horror and then he swiftly scraped along on his knees to the rear window, his flesh numb to the glass that dug deep into it. He could just make out a child, dangling upside down through the ever-increasing fumes that stung his watering eyes. The girl's head hung down motionless, her arms and legs pointed towards the broken glass that lay on the upside down roof of the car. He tried to pull the handle as the flames began to rise, and the sweat poured from every inch of his skin. He pulled harder and forcibly dragged the door across the tarmac, creating sparks as he did so.

He was not thinking; his actions were two steps ahead and his hands that normally shook were not shaking at all. The flames expanded as the screams got louder. He crawled into the back of the car. He got closer to the girl and for a second could not tell if she was alive or dead. He pulled himself nearer to her and his dread began to mount. Then he noticed her shallow breathing and his doubts turned to relief.

James unclipped the girl's seatbelt, taking care not to let her lifeless body drop onto the shards of broken glass. With both arms he steadied her and pulled her towards his chest. He now had her in his arms, and he dug his heels into anything that would give him a good grip and he pulled himself and the girl out of the car. Turning his head in order to manoeuvre his body into a better position, he noticed through the window the woman in the other car and the two pieces of amazingly unbroken glass almost touching. He now realized even more what he had to do.

People started to gather. It seemed as if every single one of them was frantically using their mobile phone. Two women took the girl from James's bleeding arms. His knees were covered with broken glass and blood seeped through the denim and down his leg.

"Cover your face!" he shouted and then kicked hard against the nearly broken window.

He had no time to check the door; it looked too buckled to open anyway. A man appeared seemingly out of nowhere and helped as James began to drag the woman from the burning wreck. He fell back and onto the street only to get straight back up again and continue with the rescue. Another man approached and took over, leaving James to run around to the other car. He could clearly see the young woman, her body pressed tightly against the now boiling hot windscreen. Her skin began to blister as the fire roared louder.

More people began to assemble. In groups, they started to try to put the fire out but they tried in vain. The burning gases turned into an ocean of orange, red and yellow, with the colours melting into each other producing a liquid that dripped from its tip and back into the engine. Each rescuer took a step back. They knew, without a single word uttered between them, the almost certain outcome: the car could explode at any moment.

James did not stop to think about this awful prospect. He strained to pull open the passenger door. His strength began to deplete. He put his fingers over the rim of the car door and down into the narrow gap that the impact had created. He pulled as hard as he could, eventually opening the door. Bizarrely, James noticed that the radio was still playing; the only device, it seemed, that was still working. The front of the car had been violently thrust back and the foot well had disappeared, leaving him not much room for movement.

"Can you move?" he called out.

There was no answer. He saw that the woman's naked left foot was trapped between the driver's door and the seat. He sat on the passenger seat and threw his legs across the car. He pushed hard against the driver's door and dislodged her foot. The woman's inert body fell back as her leg stretched, her foot thumping to the floor. James caught her falling body and then felt the raw skin on her back, her blood now on his fingers.

The fire cascaded down the window and the heat was now unbearable. With each effort to escape the car becoming harder than the last, James dug deep and fought hard before finally managing to free the woman from the blazing car. He heard the sound of sirens in the distance as he lay back on the petrol-soaked concrete. It was a sound that he had been hoping to hear for the last 10 minutes. His knees pointed up to the sky as he breathed in deeply with relief.

He waited for a while. He wanted to see if the woman would gain consciousness. He then felt a sharp stabbing pain span across his right hand and saw blood streaming from his palm and down each finger. The wound was deep. He had not noticed until he had time to stop and think about himself. He pulled off his jumper and wrapped it tightly around the gash. He did not want to hang about and was about to leave when he noticed the young woman waking up. He nervously started to walk over to her. He did not want thanks or praise. He did not feel like a hero; he had just done what he thought he had to do. As the woman was lifted into the ambulance she noticed James walking towards her. He did not know why he was walking in her direction, he just felt compelled to do so.

"Wait," she asked the paramedics.

James stopped by her side and looked into her eyes.

"Was it you?" she asked.

He just nodded and quietly said, "Yes," as he stared humbly down at the pavement.

"What's your name?"

She then noticed the blood soaking into his grey jumper, his makeshift bandage. She looked away only for a second, but by the time she turned back James had gone. She never had time to thank him, but she knew that she would never forget his face.

As he walked away he took another look at his injured hand. It began to shake. He looked at his left hand and that one was starting to shake, too. He stretched his fingers, clenching and unclenching his hands, but he could do nothing to stop the tremors. He carried on walking; he wanted to get away from the area as quickly as possible. Then he noticed the young girl and her mother being treated by the paramedics. The woman's legs were covered in blood and James could see a bone protruding agonizingly from her thigh. She was not bothered about herself, though, now that her daughter was awake and safe. James slipped behind the ambulance and away from it all, getting further and further away until he could hear nothing but silence.

Once he was back in his hotel room, James sat down at the end of the bed. As he raised his head he could see himself in the mirror. His hair was drenched in sweat, his face full of dirt. It was then that he started to realize what he had just done, and how he could quite easily not be sat there staring at his own reflection now. How lucky he had been, that time was on all their sides when it needed to be. He took off his torn clothes and threw them to the floor. He then turned on the shower and stepped in. The warm water gently cleansed his skin and washed away the drying blood that covered his knees, leaving behind just a few cuts. His hand, however, would need more than just a shower, he observed wryly.

After drying off James ripped up his worn work shirt at the sleeve and pulled it over his swelling hand, promising himself that he would get it seen to the next day. He never uttered a word of that night, not even to his wife. He did not want her to know that he had risked his life, potentially leaving his two children fatherless and Jenny a widow. To him, the people in those cars were a parent, child, or sister to somebody. Their lives were no less important than his. The cut he simply put down to a jutting out nail on a fixture at work.

*****

In the months that followed there was not a day that went by that he did not think about that night. His whole life seemed to have been a series of events; events that always seemed to put him in the right place at the right time, leading him here now. Since the day that he had been admitted into hospital all those years ago he had had a feeling that something big was going to happen one day – a sense that he had been born into this world for a reason. This was that reason, to save the lives of those people.

Seeing what he had seen had given him a high regard for life. Maybe if he had not gone through what he had then he, too, would have been one of those people who just stood and watched as the cars went up in flames. But James did not think about it. His mind was set and his instinct took over. The voice that he had heard so many times was no longer there but he never stopped feeling that he was still being helped or guided in one way or another.

Then, as always, James started to delve more into his thoughts, more into the reasoning behind everything. Why him? Why did it need to be him? Was he missing something? Who were the people that he had saved? Were they, too, a part of something bigger? He rehashed everything over and over again in his mind. He had played his part but he needed to know *why* this had happened. Did everybody follow a path, or was he just one of a few? Is everybody part of the same plan? The possibility seemed too extreme, and too surreal.

Maybe those people had been pulled from the car for the same reason that he had been in hospital. Maybe at a later time they would also be in a situation to save somebody or help somebody, with each event following on to the next. These happenings, these events, could only be a small factor in something a lot bigger – something more complicated… not that this was not complicated enough!

He thought about everything in great detail, as he always did. He went through his whole life, as much as he could remember, one last time, to try to come up with an answer. If he had not banged his head then he would have probably died soon after. But he *did* bang his head on that day – at that time, at that exact second. It all could not have been just a coincidence that Daniel had turned up that day. What made him decide to go and play football? Maybe James was reading too much into it all, but he just could not help himself.

Each time he thought about it hard enough he almost came up with the answer only to think of something else that did not quite add up sending his whole train of thought into chaos, each explanation contradicting the next. He did believe, though, that he could not be the only one and that, although he was in a way being guided, he knew that he was free to make all of his own decisions. He had free will, it was all him. He just needed to know *why* he was in certain places at certain times.

The whole experience of being in hospital and learning the value of life had made him the man he was now, and that man had saved those people from that car crash. If he had not had the brain tumour then he would have followed a whole different career path, he would never have had that amazing phone call and met Jenny and he would never have had his children. His whole life would have been completely different.

James walked into the living room, his thoughts still ticking over. Plonking himself down on the light tan leather settee and leaning back, he felt a lump underneath the cushion. Feeling underneath, he found a toy tank that Callum had been playing with that very morning. Like a bolt of lightning, a memory flashed in his mind – something that his mum had told him years ago; something that he had forgotten; something that might help him understand.

His mother had told him a story about her grandfather – something that had happened in the First World War. He had been picked out to be in the first tank of about four. As he prepared to climb in he remembered that he had forgotten something. His mother did not know what this something was, but he was allowed to go back and get whatever it was. The first tank left without him and somebody from the back tank went in his place. He, in turn, took the last tank. As they all took off that day the tank that his mother's grandfather was meant to be in was blown up and everybody in it was killed instantly. James's great-grandfather had been saved.

Was this luck or was this, again, another moment in the greater scheme of things? What had made him forget something that was so important? If he had not forgotten it then, ultimately, James would never have been born. His grandmother would never have been born! Was his great-grandfather saved that day so eventually James

191

was to be born and he would be there that night in Birmingham? Did it go back that far or even further? If it was possible to investigate his whole family tree, down to the smallest decisions, what would he find? What would anybody find if they did the same?

Who was the soldier that took his place in the tank? Why did he have to die? This was one of the parts that James could not understand. Why does anybody have to die in a tragic way? Surely he was not sacrificed so that James's family could continue to grow? Or was it simply just meant to be? His time was up but James's great-grandfather's was not?

Are things really mapped out this way before anybody is even born? Does someone up there know the time and day of everyone's death? Do they know about everyone's future? James liked to think they did not, but his experiences told him different.

James was aware that most people could have the same sort of story. If their parents had not met, what then? He knew also that he had seen miraculous escapes that people had had on the telly. For example: "*If she had been in the road a split second later then she would have been killed!*"

Everyone has heard or seen something like this, but James's question was *why*? Was it just pure luck or was it meant to be? Was it a bit of both or nothing at all? Was something, or someone, helping these people, just like James had been? The only difference was that James had been given proof that he was being helped, but whose voice was it? And why did she let herself be known?

After a lot of thinking and wondering James had to concede that some things are not meant to be understood. What he *did* believe was this: he was only one of many, if not everybody in the world, who is playing their part. Everyone, in one way or another, is connected to everyone else, somehow. Everyone on this planet is here for a reason, each person bringing their own meaning to the world.

We should all be here to help one another and if we need a little bit of guidance along the way then so be it. We are all given the tools to take different directions in life. Some choose to use them and some do not. Sometimes, however, and in certain parts of their lives, those choices are made for them – people just do not necessarily know it.

Chapter 10

2010

James's dad had come up with the idea of taking his two sons over to France for a weekend. His plan was to go to Vimy Ridge and see the memorial; something he had done with his own father and brother many years ago and something that he had spoken often about doing with his own children.

James and Chris's plans, though, were slightly different from their dad's: theirs involved a bit of drinking along the way. Of course, they *were* interested in seeing the sights with their old man but there was nothing wrong with a bit of alcohol mixed in.

Having his usual connections, their dad had managed to wangle a cottage for the weekend. Parking the car outside the cottage after a ferry ride and the drive that followed, all three looked at their accommodation for the first time. Opening the creaking door, and noticing the disarray that lay before them, Chris dropped his bag, almost disgusted that this was the place that he would have to sleep.

"Is this it?" he asked.

"I told you it hadn't been finished yet, Chris," replied his dad.

"Finished… finished… It hasn't even been started, by the look of things! Good friend of yours, was he, that loaned you his place, is he?" Chris asked, the disappointment evident in his tone of voice.

"Yes he is, Chris. You can always sleep in the car, if you want."

"Dad, that's actually very tempting, but I'll rough it for a while at first, don't worry!"

The place looked as though it had only been half built; the wrong half, it seemed. They now knew why their dad had been so insistent on them all bringing a good sleeping bag. This was because there was no proper heating, with only a little log fire that looked as though it would fall apart at the slightest touch. Any bit of warmth it may generate, though, would probably only escape through the gaps in the poorly fitted windows. There was no wood anyway, even if they had wanted to start a fire.

Looking down at his sleeping bag, James thought it might be warmer if he slept outside and it crossed his mind that he should have brought a tent as well.

"Pub!" shouted Chris, ignoring any idea of work that he might have to do in order to get the dilapidated building even slightly warm.

"I agree. Come on, Dad. We can get some wood on the way back," James called out.

Chris was the last one out of the cottage so he pulled the door shut behind him.

"Erm, Dad? Was the door knob meant to come off?" he called out.

Having tried to secure it back on the door and not succeeding, he decided to throw it to the ground and fix it later instead.

They had not been walking for long down the old country lane when they came across a small village pub. They made their way up the old worn and dipped concrete steps, with Chris leading the way. He gently pulled open the wooden door, being careful not to pull too hard on the handle this time. The pub was almost empty. The only two customers that were already in there turned and watched as they made their entrance.

For someone who had failed dismally at French at school, Chris seemed confident in his ability to speak the language. It did seem, however, that it would not be long until the whole range of his lingual ability would become quite apparent.

"Bonjour, bonjour," he said as he made his way through the room and into the bar. "What are you having, you two? The first round's on–"

Chris's offer of a drink was distracted by the arrival of a gorgeous barmaid who had just appeared from a room behind the bar and was walking towards them. Chris seemed to understand her arrival, though, as being purely for him.

"Bonjour," was said one more time but this was quickly followed by his native tongue. "Do you speak English?" he asked.

"Non," she replied with a smile; a smile that Chris again misunderstood as her eyelashes fluttered in his general direction.

"James, you'd better order the drinks," he said, his eyes locked onto his latest conquest-to-be.

James tried as best he could but only knew just a few more French words than his brother did. He did know, however, that *petite* meant 'small' and this was a size of drink that they did not want. He opted for the next choice which was *grande*. Happy in their decision, they watched as the barmaid walked to the other side of the bar and picked up three very large pint glasses – or, rather, three very large three-pint glasses. It took both hands just to lift the glasses up but once they did the lager flowed nicely. Before they knew it, several hours had slipped past and it was getting late.

Chris, proving once again to be ever the ladies' man, was hitting on the barmaid whilst James was trying to keep his dad sitting upright on the stool. The place seemed a lot busier now as each hour merged into the next. The misunderstood singing, tunes that they recognized but lyrics that they did not, added to the atmosphere of a drunken bar.

"Dad... Dad, sit up straight," James said, propping up his sozzled father while his own ability to sit without falling off his own stool became increasingly more of a challenge.

"Chris, we have to go. I can't hold him up anymore. I can barely sit on my own stool. Come on, let's go," James managed to call out over his giggles.

Chris turned around and through his drunken teeth hissed at James, "Can't you see I'm busy? *You* take him back."

"Chris, he's six-foot-three and as drunk as a skunk. This is going to take the both of us to get him back."

"Come on, James, just another hour, *please,*" he pleaded, choosing still not to take his eyes off the barmaid.

"We can come back tomorrow, Chris."

Chris turned and held the barmaid's hand and gently pulled it up to his mouth.

"Chris, pucker down and let's go – *now!*" James said with urgency.

"Hang on, James, just give me a sec."

"Chris, step away from the woman," James warned.

Chris turned around and snapped back at James, "Will you stop nagging, please! I won't be long."

"Did she happen to tell you whether she was married in any shape or form, Chris?"

"For God's sake, why?"

James pointed to a rather large Frenchman dressed in a bloodied apron and pushing his way through anything and anyone that got in his way.

"That's why! I can't speak French that well, my stupid brother, but I *can* tell you that when a man is growling, snorting, and grunting, and making his way angrily towards you it's understandable in *any* language... so let's just go!"

James started to drag his father from the stool as his brother quickly attempted to do the same, but each time they managed to get him to his feet he slipped from their grasp and slumped back down again.

"Let's just leave him."

"Chris, we are not leaving him here. Just grab him again."

Both again tugged at their father's flapping arms, but it was too late. The macho chef had arrived and was standing directly behind Chris and towering over him. The words that left his mouth were indeed French, but not the sort of French that Chris and James had failed to learn at school.

"I can explain," said Chris, holding his hands up in the air.

"Unless you have managed to learn French in the last three hours, Chris, I don't think you will be explaining anything, anytime soon," James said ruefully.

A little, old French man approached and declared that he could speak English. His translations, however, only seemed to make everyone in the pub roar with laughter and anger the barmaid's husband even more.

"Chris, just grab Dad and let's at least get out the door."

Together they pulled their father one more time from the stool and dragged him towards the exit, escaping a situation that was more than certainly about to turn nasty. Still, though, as they struggled up the slight incline towards the cold, musty cottage they began to laugh at the whole situation. Remembering that he had dropped the doorknob on the ground, Chris began searching where it may have fallen.

"Can you hold Dad for a minute while I find the knob, James?" he asked, but not giving his brother enough notice before he bent down to the ground.

Losing his grip on their father, James accidently let go, leaving his dad to fall slowly, but blissfully unaware, onto the grass behind him. James could do nothing but watch and hope that he did not hit anything hard on his way down. Finding the knob, Chris again tried to fix it to the door – this time wishing that he had taken the time to mend it when it had fallen off earlier. Holding it in place and ready to turn as soon as the door was unlocked he turned to his brother and asked, "You got the key, James?"

"No, I thought you had it."

"I'm not going back to that bar, James. No way! Right, that's it... I'm kicking down the door!" he declared, lifting his leg and preparing himself.

"Don't be stupid. Dad's got them, I bet. Check his pockets."

After a few seconds of searching their father's dead-to-the-world body, Chris managed to retrieve the key and unlocked the door. He considered throwing a sleeping bag over their father and leaving him outside for the rest of the night, but his conscience must have got the better of him, though, as he began to lift his dad up, with the help of James, and into the cottage.

"Where are the lights? I can't see a thing," James said.

Taking a few steps into the darkness, Chris yelped with pain.

"What is it, Chris?"

"It's okay. It's only the camp bed. Let's put Dad down here and find the switch."

Together they lowered their dad gently down onto the camp bed and, knowing he was now safe, went in search of the light switch.

"Got it!" Chris shouted through the dark and started to flick it on and off.

"Damn, the fuse has gone," he muttered.

Remembering that his phone had a torch on it, Chris began to look for the fuse box. Once the fuse box was found and switches fiddled with, Chris flicked on the lights. Success! He seemed almost impressed with his own achievement. The room was now lit but the view was not in the slightest any better than they remembered it the first time they walked in.

"Where's Dad?" asked James.

Both he and Chris scanned the room quickly. Their drunken father was nowhere to be seen.

"You had him last, Chris."

"What do you mean *I* had him last, James? We *both* had him! He can't have just vanished!"

"Do you think he walked out when we were looking for the fuse box?"

"Don't be stupid, James. He couldn't even stand let alone walk anywhere in the state that he was in."

"Shh! I hear something," Chris said, pointing at the camp bed.

As they neared it the drunken groans got louder. They could not understand how their dad had fallen into the impossible gap in-between the bed and the wall and then managed, somehow, to actually be *underneath* the bed, his face showing an almost childish grin as he grumbled and snored. Chris and James began to laugh out loud, their voices echoing through the empty shell of a building. Pulling him from the floor and into the living area, they made him as warm and as comfortable as they could and left him to sleep it off on the old, lumpy settee.

"I'll take the camp bed out here, James. Where are you sleeping?"

"I'll just sleep in the chair and sort out something better for tomorrow night," he replied, pointing to the high backed chair in the corner of the room.

After just a few hours of sleep James was woken by a light that blazed through the living room door, hurting his sensitive eyes as it did so. He just about managed to make out an outline: a silhouette of a shivering figure. At first he panicked and started to pull his sleeping bag over his head but on a second glance he could see that it was his brother in his boxer shorts. He stood there shivering with what looked like some sort of flannel, a small blanket at best.

"It's fr-fr-freezing out th-there a-and I f-f-for-g-got m-my s-sleep-p-ping b-bag," he stammered as he walked towards his brother. "D-do y-you r-reckon D-dad w-will n-notice if I t-take h-his?"

James started to laugh. The whole night had been one long laugh. Chris, having forgotten the one thing that had been drummed into him, added to the funny memories of a lager-infused weekend. At that point they both looked down at their dad and wondered if he would notice if they did, indeed, take away his only source of warmth. It was at that exact point that their dad lifted his head and promptly vomited all over the antique rug, the sheer volume of his wretches probably waking up any French person within a two-mile radius.

"Sorry, lads," he mumbled and then promptly rolled back over to sleep.

"I'm not cleaning that up, Chris!"

"Nor me! Dad can do it in the morning," stated Chris, covering his nose from the smell of vomit mixed with alcohol.

After the sick had been cleaned up the following morning, and after 20 minutes of trying to convince their still slightly drunken Dad that cutting a hole in the rug probably was not the best idea, they all made their way to the old battlefields of the Somme.

The whole trip was humbling for them all, thinking about all those British and Commonwealth soldiers who died during the battles that happened there. The sheer amount of white gravestones, some with names but plenty with just the words '*a British soldier*' or '*an Australian soldier*', was very sad to see. The tunnels that were built by the New Zealand soldiers went on for what seemed like miles. The stories they read about in the museum were nothing short of unbelievable. Enemies in trenches that where only yards away was one of the things that James found hard to believe. Even to this day visitors to the area are not allowed to walk on the grass in case there are unexploded mines that lie in wait: a cruel intent that hadn't been fulfilled nearly one hundred years before. Chris, James, and their dad all agreed that what those soldiers went through was horrendous. Their drunken antics from the night before were forgotten momentarily as they remembered the men and women who gave their lives so that future generations could have theirs.

James left France that weekend being thankful for the era he had been born in. He was not so sure how he would have coped having to go to war. But then again, nobody knows what their reactions would be to any given situation until it happens.

Chapter 11

2010

Since James had become a parent, life seemed to zoom by. Before he knew it, his children had reached the ages of 12 and 14. He was now happily married and his relationship had blossomed into something better than perfection. Money was not as big a problem as it used to be and things were better than ever. Together, James and Jenny had built something beautiful. They had managed to buy their own house with a little bit of help from their parents: a house that they took pride in and worked hard to maintain.

On the morning of March the 18th 2010, two days before Ben's 13th birthday, James was in his local supermarket searching for party banners in celebration of his son's milestone – reaching his teens. He spotted the perfect banner; the last one in the shop, it seemed. Reaching up above the greetings cards and gift bags, he managed to get a hold of it between two fingers, his other hand still holding onto the shopping basket. He could not get a good enough grip and had to let go. He needed both his hands. He bent over and placed the shopping basket on the floor, but on his way back up he closed his eyes and scrunched up his face in agony. A pulsating tension passed through the side of his head and blackness covered the lower part of his decreasing vision. He tried to hold his head up with both his hands pressing his fingers into his skull. And then, nothing: the pain just simply vanished. He paused a moment and contemplated leaving the banner and basket where they were; he was too scared to bend over again. He did not want the aching drill to repeat itself. He waited for a few minutes and then swiftly picked up the basket, bending as little as possible and keeping his head up, and carried on his shopping, keeping in mind the entire time what had just happened.

Days went past and nothing: not a pain, not an ache, not even a mild twinge. The more time that went past the more James put the headache down to a one-off. He could not, and would not, live life in fear of another brain tumour. He reassured himself that he, too, could get normal headaches just like everyone else.

It was almost two months that had passed before he found himself lying on the garage floor. He could not remember falling and he could not recall banging his head on the way down. Wiping away the blood with the back of his hand, he started to pull himself up with the help of the nearby stepladder. He instantly felt a surging pain travel from the back of his skull to the front above his eyes and again he plummeted backwards. Another attempt and he managed to get to his feet.

A few weeks later and the attacks were becoming more frequent. James kept them to himself: a stupid attempt not to worry his family. He knew that he would have to tell Jenny at some point but he just did not know how. He carried on as if things were normal, as if he was not experiencing these blackouts, headaches, and loss of balance. Things went from bad to worse until one night he was lying in bed, his head immersed between his two pillows, when the ringing in his ears began to peel like thunder. He clawed at the pillows in a panic and moved them away from his head.

"Jenny, Jenny! Wake up!"

He nudged her until she rolled over and began the conversation he had never intended having with his wife. She sat up and started to cry, the tears being the beginning of many.

James had to undergo a series of tests the same as before. This time, however, he felt a lot more vulnerable. He had maturity this time, a better understanding of the situation, and a lot more to lose. The terminology was not censored to protect him anymore. Although his thoughts had taken him back to that of a 14-year-old boy, he was not. He was now a man and he was treated like one, but how he wished he was not!

His eyes were checked with an ophthalmoscope, an instrument he had seen before but had never heard the name before. It was a tool that shone a light into the backs of his eyes to see if there was any swelling known as a papilloedema. He had hearing tests, facial muscle tests, and his reflexes were examined. The pattern began and history repeated itself. Deep down inside, he knew what was happening. It was not long before he and Jenny were in the hospital waiting room. James was next in line for another CT scan, an event he had wished that would never happen again. Memories began to haunt his mind and the clinical smell that was once a thing of the past bore deep into his waking nightmare.

"Mr Squires, can you come through," came the voice of the radiographer, and the start of another daunting journey.

James stood up and walked the blue carpet for what seemed like forever until he reached the large, white machine once again. This time, lying still as instructed was much harder than before. Each familiar sound caused his body to jerk, shake, and jolt.

"Try to keep still, James," said a voice through the clicking intercom.

He kept his head still as best he could until it was all over. Then all he had to do was wait. Wait two anxious days before he was called back for the results.

"Hello, James. Do take a seat. I'm Mr Banks. You obviously know why you're here today."

His manner was serious and his body language did not show much promise of anything positive to come. James sat and listened; the words were familiar, but the whole situation strangely surreal.

"I've had a look at the results and I have to tell you it's not good news."

Jenny, who was sitting next to her husband, held his hand tighter, the news smashing all her positive feelings as her heart sank.

"You have a primary brain tumour situated in the same place as before – the cerebellum. It's seldom that this type of tumour grows back, but, in your case, I'm afraid it has."

Mr Banks waited for a response, but James again just listened, and Jenny said nothing either.

"The good news is that because of your history it's likely to be a Grade One growth. We won't know for sure until we've done more tests."

"What happens next?" Jenny asked with a desperate need for knowledge, her fingers wiping away yet more tears.

211

"Well, I want to do another scan: this time an MRI. This will give us a clearer picture of what we are dealing with, along with the CT scan that's just been done. We can then decide the best course of treatment."

"Thank you."

That was all James could say as he stood up and shook the registrar's hand. He and Jenny left the room in shocked silence.

More time went by and things moved much slower now that James was an adult. He knew that he had a brain tumour and he just wanted to get rid of it. He realized that no matter what kind of tumour it was, his recovery period would be a lot longer and twice as hard. He was older. He was no longer the fit, athletic teenager he was the first time round. If he was to go through the hours of surgery again, the weeks that he had spent in the children's hospital would probably turn into months this time. The one thing he did have still was his family. The family who would help him through this, the family that was now bigger and stronger who would provide strength when he needed it most.

Chapter 12

2010

"Good job today, Sam. We're going to miss you."

"Thanks, Clive. I will miss you all, too."

Sam had returned to Birmingham to continue her research into childhood leukaemia; a job that she was committed to and that had taken her all over the world. Every posting gave her a new understanding of the illness and more knowledge on how best to treat it. Today was her last day at the Queen Elizabeth Hospital in Birmingham. She had spent her last two months dividing her time between Birmingham University, the children's hospital, and, of course, the QE. The Queen Elizabeth and the university were two of the world's leading researchers in breakthrough treatment for the disease that Sam had dedicated her life to researching.

She was good at her job. Many doctors asked for her opinion. She was still only 31, but she had already gained a great deal of respect from most of her colleagues and doctors that had been treating cancer for a lot longer than she had. She had the drive and passion that was needed to be the best. Her ideas and suggestions were always considered as genuine possibilities.

After a long day, Sam made her way to the staffroom with a spring in her step. She poured herself a drink from the water cooler with excitement and looked forward to seeing her family back in America. For the past two months she had only had contact through the latest technology, something that was not quite the same as holding someone and chatting to them face to face. She also missed the Sunday lunches that were spent around the dining table at her family home, the smells from the kitchen as her mother served up her favourite dishes, the laughter, and the odd glass of wine. In short, Sam missed home.

Making her way to the women's changing rooms she stopped and noticed an envelope on the coffee table. It was addressed to her: a card from all the staff that she had worked with over the last eight weeks. Smiling, she continued over to her locker and pulled it open revealing a photo of her mother, father, and sister stuck neatly to the inside of the door; a photo she took with her wherever she went.

She then began to remove her scrubs. Putting her hands behind her, she pulled at the collar and slid it over her head. As the top moved up her back a scar began to emerge, running from the centre right side and just above her right shoulder blade. A scar that reminded her every day of how lucky she was that night when she was saved by a mysterious man.

As she walked the floors of the hospital one last time, she was stopped by a colleague who she had met during her training back in 1997 – someone who she had met up with numerous times during her travels.

"Keep in touch, Sam. Remember, I'll see you next year," she said.

"Are you coming over then, Jane? I didn't know!" Sam replied, a sarcastic quip referring to the amount of times that the trip had been mentioned.

As Sam moved in to give her friend a farewell hug she paused, her distraction noticed by Jane as she withdrew from the embrace. Her right hand was still on Jane's shoulder, gently moving across her front as she started to walk in awe towards what she had just seen. Walking slowly at first, she eagerly started to follow the hospital bed that had just passed her in the corridor. Her stride became faster and her heart began to pound.

She placed her left hand on the anaesthetist's shoulder and slowed him down to a stop. Ignoring him, she moved around the bed and looked at the patient's face. She recognized him in an instant. Before her was the man who had saved her life. The young man had now aged a few years, but it was definitely him. She noticed immediately the scar on his right hand. If she had been unsure before, she was not now.

"Hi, what's your name?" she asked, a question that had never been answered.

"James," he replied, knowing exactly who this woman was but not needing to voice his recognition.

Sam placed her hand over her mouth and while choking back her tears she simply said, "Thank you."

Noticing Jenny, she stepped out of the way of the bed and watched as James was taken to his destination. Her eyes never left him as he was wheeled around the corner.

***

"Okay, James, you're going to feel a little prick."

James smiled to himself and remembered the similar conversation before.

"James, when I say, can you start to count back from ten."

As James began to count he was interrupted by a voice; not just *any* voice but the voice that he had not heard for 20 years. He lifted his head slightly and started to whisper something to the anaesthetist. The voice spoke through the numbers and long after he had fallen asleep she carried on talking to him, reassuring him in his dreams.

Jenny and Sam were sitting quietly in the waiting room when the anaesthetist walked in.

"Don't worry, everything's fine. James asked me to tell you something, Sam. He said that he's asked the question and it's not time. That's all he said," he relayed, looking somewhat puzzled.

Sam could do nothing but smile.

The End